Bad Boyfriend

A TRUE STORY OF 90S CLUB KIDS

NORMAN FOX

Copyright 2025 © Norman Fox

ISBN: 978-0-646-71079-2

AUTHOR'S NOTE

This story is based on my personal experiences. The names and the identifying char-acteristics of the people who appear in this story have been altered and some charac-ters have been combined. Certain events and situations have also been imaginatively transformed, and those events and situations are not intended to portray actual events and situations.

Please be aware that this story contains content that may be distressing and triggering for some people. If you need assistance or support, please contact the following:

Beyond Blue on 1300 22 4636 or beyondflue.org.au, or

Lifeline on 13 11 14 or lifeline.org.au

I dedicate this book to my husband, Stephen, and to Oxford Street in the 90s. The golden gay mile where I met my Mr Right.

PROLOGUE

ON THE RECORD

CURIOUS, I PRESSED play on my cassette recorder…
'The time is 5:45pm on November 27, 1991. I'm plainclothes Constable First Class Ferguson, and this is Detective Brown seated opposite me. Mr James, I am going to ask you some questions about credit card number 5353 1234 4321 0987, that was stolen from the Darlinghurst branch and about 23 credit card vouchers that were used to purchase over $4000 worth of goods with this stolen card. You are not obliged to say anything unless you wish to do so, but whatever you say will be electronically recorded and may be used in evidence and used against you. Do you understand that?'

'Yes, I do.'

'Just speak up.'

'YES – I DO.'

'For the purposes of this interview, what is your full name?'

'Dom, I mean – Dominic Troy James'

'What is your date of birth?'

'January 30, 1970.'

'Dominic, let's take your mind back to September. You remember being employed by the bank. What was your situation there?'

'I was employed as a teller at the Darlinghurst branch.'

'And how long had you been employed by the bank?'

'Just over 2 years.'

'I'll now show you a code of conduct interview dated October 1, 1991, that was recorded with your solicitor, Mr Steel. Would you just have a careful read through that? I'll give you a few minutes.'

A cold silence descended, apart from the sounds of pages being shuffled.

'Having read the record of interview, do you agree that this is the interview you had with your former manager, Mr Yates, on October 1, 1991?'

'Yes, as far as I'm aware, that's my signature, so that must have been the one.'

'Was any threat, promise, or inducement offered to you to give any of the answers contained in that interview?'

'No, not that I'm aware of.'

'Did you participate in the interview of your own free will?'

'Yes, I did.'

'Are the answers as given by you in that interview true, and correct?'

'Um, yes, as far as I can remember.'

'Is there anything further you would like to say about the record of interview?'

'Um n-no. Sorry, yes there is. The fact is, at the time I made the interview, I was in a very mentally unstable state and quite distraught, so, therefore, anything that I said could have been a stress reaction.'

'So, are you saying it's not accurate? Did you lie?'

'I'm not saying I lied or anything. I'm just saying I don't recall the total content of the interview due to my mental state.'

'Dom, now that you've read the interview again today, are you satisfied that the answers you gave are accurate?'

'As far as to what I remember, yes.'

Detective Brown asked his first question to Dom since the interview started, *'Okay, so what you're basically telling us is that when you took part in the interview, you were under a fair amount of stress?'*

'Yes, I was very distraught,' Dom admitted.

As I listened, I wondered which of the two policemen were playing the 'bad cop'. Both sounded robotic, unimpressed, and their tone indicated they thought Dom was guilty.

'But to the best of your knowledge, the answers you gave are true and correct.'

'Yes, as best as I can remember.'

'Now, I draw your attention to a card marked 5353 1234 4321 0987 for a Sheba Krishnan. What can you tell me about that card?'

'That was the card Tiffany used on that morning.'

'I now draw your attention to a copy of a release form and the column marked Card Holder Signature. What can you tell me about the signature that appears there?'

'That the signature is S Krishnan.'

'Who signed that?'

'Tiffany.'

'Tiffany who?'

'Tiffany Anderson.'

'What can you tell me about Tiffany?'

'Tiffany was my flat mate when I lived in Surry Hills.'

I still couldn't believe my best friend since primary school had involved us in this.

'Did you make any arrangements with Tiffany prior to coming into the bank in relation to that card? Did you have any discussion?'

'Yes. She said she'd done it before and that we wouldn't get caught.'

'Can you tell me who handed out that card?'

'I gave that card to Tiffany.'

'So, Tiffany is not, in fact, this Sheba Krishnan person, the name on the credit card?'

'No, no, she was not.'

'And, obviously, no identification was produced to you in order for you to hand the card over.'

'No, there wasn't.'

'And that is not the usual bank policy?'

'No, it's not.'

'Can you tell me, when you handed that card to Tiffany, were you aware that she was not entitled to take possession of that card?'

'Yes, I was.' Dom let out a shaky breath.

'Can you tell me that when you handed that same card to Tiffany, bearing in mind you were aware that she was not entitled to take possession of that card. Was Tiffany also aware that she was not entitled to take possession of that card?'

'Yes.'

'Thank you.'

SOBER

NEW YEAR'S EVE 1990, THE HORDERN PAVILION, SYDNEY, AUSTRALIA

ON A SPECIAL night like New Year's Eve, it was perfectly acceptable to approach complete strangers for a French kiss, provided you'd taken the right dose of drugs. Depending on the combination of chemicals in your system, it felt like you could break all the rules. Suddenly, a stranger could become your long-lost best friend under the mirror-balls. This is what happened when Tiffany and I locked eyes for the first time in over a year.

I got the feeling Tiffany couldn't believe what her euphorically dilated pupils were seeing across the sweat-soaked stadium. There I was. Her ex-boyfriend. Tiffany's first love. Someone Tiffany now resented because I'd stopped talking to her for over a year.

I grooved to the beats of 'Dirty Cash (Money Talks)' by The Adventures of Stevie V and pretended not to see Tiffany. I was in no mood to get caught up in an ugly dance party reunion scene. But Tiffany kept staring at me.

I knew I looked flawless, even though I was covered in perspiration. My jet-black hair was gelled perfectly, like Elvis Presley's. Tiffany once told me she didn't know how I managed to keep my hair perfectly styled while sweating it out with six thousand other 'drug-fucked' individuals. Not a strand was out of place as I moved energetically to the beat of house music. Like most gay men, I had an impeccable sense of style, wearing the latest underground retro fashion trend, a flamboyant psychedelic 60s shirt. I looked like a member of the one-hit-wonder dance music group Dee-Lite, and groove was in my heart. I was the kind of boy who stood out from the crowd.

As I danced with my high school buddies, we grinned at each other. We'd all clocked Tiffany and pretended not to see her. We were having the time of our lives along with several thousand other smiling faces surrounding us. The Hordern was full of love, smiles, and arms stretching up to the pulsating laser lights.

From the corner of my eye, I noticed Tiffany stray from her friends and move towards us. On illicit substances, Tiffany and I had frequently mistaken complete strangers for people we thought we knew. I could tell Tiffany was hoping that this wasn't the case as she pushed through the mass of sweaty bodies towards me.

'Nathan!' Tiffany yelled at the top of her lungs. 'Happy New Year!' She planted a giant French kiss on my lips.

'Tiffany! Oh my God, I thought you were dead!' I pretended to be thrilled as I squeezed Tiffany's skinny body close to mine. 'What are you doing in Sydney?'

'I live here now. I'm in a band. We're recording a demo for Central Station Records!'

'Bullshit! When did all this happen?'

'Oh, about the same time you stopped talking to me!'

'Wait a minute. You stopped talking to me.'

'No way!' Tiffany insisted but being high and feeling ecstatic she let this potential disagreement go without starting an argument. 'It's good to see you, darling.' Tiffany smiled. She was still as attractive as ever.

'You too, Tiffany. I should have guessed I'd see you again on the dance floor!' I grinned, feeling no apology was needed for losing touch.

'So, what have you taken tonight?' Tiffany got straight down to business.

'Nothing.'

'Couldn't you score?'

'It's not that.'

It was my first dance party since completing the High School Certificate, the dreaded HSC. I hadn't taken any drugs to celebrate. For the first time in a long time, I was dancing on a natural high. I'd given up drugs to concentrate on getting an impressive HSC score.

'My friends have some pills if you want?' Tiffany offered.

'It's cool. I'm just happy being here.'

'Really?' Being high on her chemical wings, Tiffany couldn't comprehend the revelation that I was sober. In fact, in her state of mind, I suspected it was hard to comprehend much at all. I knew Tiffany well. She once said that attending a dance party and not being on drugs was incomprehensible. In Tiffany's altered reality, dance parties and drugs went hand in hand. Everybody knew that! She'd insisted on this whenever we were high together as seventeen-years-olds.

Realising that I was not joking about being sober at a dance party, Tiffany could only think of one thing to say, 'What happened to you, Nathan? You used to be cool!'

'So, what have you taken?' I asked, looking into Tiffany's giant black pupils.

'I popped an E, dropped a trip, and blasted speed.'

I was shocked and surprised to hear Tiffany admit she'd *blasted speed*. I knew this was code for injecting it, using a needle, something I believed only serious drug addicts or junkies did. In my mind, this meant Tiffany had crossed a line from recreational user to serious addiction. 'You blasted speed?'

'Oh, for sure man!' Tiffany nodded enthusiastically. 'It's much cleaner than snorting it!'

I was taken aback and concerned at the casual way Tiffany rationalised injecting drugs, claiming it was *'cleaner'*. This made me recall how, the last time I saw Tiffany, at a dingy nightclub in Kings Cross, I'd overdosed at age seventeen thanks to her influence. Even in those days, I never went near a needle. I was scared to and hated the idea of needles. No high was worth track marks. Or worse.

I was a different person to the boy Tiffany had partied with in the 80s. Now it was the first day of 1991. I was enjoying the thrill of being back inside Club Hordern. It was amazing to see that the RAT parties were still attracting the crowds, twenty thousand people to be exact. Like many revellers, Tiffany's eyes were bulging from the chemicals she'd consumed, and she chewed gum at a rapid rate. It was a familiar feeling, yet somehow something was different. The dance party, or rave scene as it was now known, had changed. For the club kids like Tiffany, it was obvious that the drugs weren't as strong as they'd first been. That's why she had resorted to blasting speed just to get the same happy high feeling she'd experienced when she had been sixteen.

What was even more disappointing for the regulars at Club Hordern was that the music was much softer than it had been in the late 80s. It was possible to hold a conversation about what drugs you'd taken while on the dance floor without having to scream the details into someone's ear. The reduced volume of the once booming house music was thanks to a consistent complaint campaign waged by the homeowners on Moore Park Road. The residents' angry letters to the local council had almost put an end to what was the heart of the Sydney dance party scene.

I decided to change the subject away from drugs to something I knew Tiffany would enjoy talking about. 'You look amazing, Tiffany!' I smiled and gave my ex-girlfriend another hug.

'Thanks, love.' Tiffany smiled at the compliment and ran her hands over her short, bleach-blond hair. It was cut short like a boy's. She wore just the right amount of makeup and was much skinnier than when I used to know her. These days, Tiffany had no problem displaying her thin body to full advantage. She wore silver hot pants, a red sequin glittery brazier, and shiny black high-heel platform boots. At eighteen-years-old, Tiffany had grown up to become a vision of perfection, a dedicated disco dolly. She was the envy of most other girls on the dance floor and caught the attention of the few strays — straight boys — among the predominately gay crowd.

'So, what are you doing in a band?' I asked.

'I do vocals. We're called Elemental, and we do happy hardcore house music!'

'Wow! I can't wait to hear your stuff.'

'Oh, for sure, man. You're going to love it. What are you doing these days?'

'Starting university.'

'Nerd!'

At that instant, an ice-cube flew between Tiffany's breasts and landed in her sequin brazier. Tiffany looked startled, and turned to see where the projectile came from. She grinned and rolled her eyes once she realised the culprit was one of her band mates.

'I think my keyboard player is getting jealous!' Tiffany laughed as she fished the ice-cube from her bra. 'You look good, Nathan. Why did we stop talking to each other?'

'I had to put the brakes on partying to get through the HSC, Tiffany. It wasn't anything personal.'

'Really?' Tiffany seemed to be less ecstatic. Even the drugs couldn't mask the fact she looked sad for a second. 'Which university are you going to?'

'University of New England.'

'Huh?'

'In Lismore.'

'Where's Lismore?'

'It's a country town in Northern New South Wales. I'm going to study Media Communications.'

'Aw. Why aren't you going to uni here?'

'Where do I start? I'm over Sydney.'

There were many reasons why I had decided to study away from home. Thanks to growing up in my parents conveniently located Eastern suburbs home, I had experimented and over-indulged during my senior high school years. I'd been a pretend straight boy on the edge, spending Saturday nights delirious under the bright lights of Club Hordern, perving at the countless muscular men on the dance floor. I'd pretended to be straight for my school friends, my best mates who had been known in the playground as The Group. It had been a confusing and tiring existence. It was this upbringing that had led me to make a deliberate choice when it came to my tertiary education. I decided to enrol in a university course located far, far away from the temptations of Sydney. At eighteen years old, I felt that I needed to make a fresh start to avoid the lure of Sydney's nightlife to concentrate on getting a passport to a better future, known as a degree.

'You're kidding, right? I can't see you in a country town, Nathan.' Tiffany frowned. 'I give you about a month before you pack your bags and come back.'

'We'll see.' I raised my brows and ignored Tiffany's words. I danced energetically, not wanting to talk anymore about my reasons for leaving.

Tiffany danced closer to me with amphetamine, MDMA, and LSD working their way through her bloodstream. I could tell the drugs were making her extra happy to see me again. She started to smile again, a perfect orthodontist-engineered smile. Tiffany mouthed the words to The Communard's 'Never can say goodbye'.

I suspected her smile was induced mainly by the drugs. Now on a special night, with the right amount of chemicals injected into her system, Tiffany was able to reconnect with me, the boy who had once been her one true love, before she'd discovered drugs.

On the first day of a new year, Tiffany and I swapped phone numbers and promised to stay in touch 'for real' this time.

SWEAT PARTY

AFTER COMPLETING THE HSC, it was time to go to university, get a job, build a career, become rich and famous, or start collecting social security and be called an Aussie dole-bludger by the Liberal Party. Those were the options when you turn eighteen years old in Australia and have your whole future ahead of you.

Before any of these scenarios became a reality, the first stop after the HSC was Schoolies week in sunny Queensland. Like all good Aussie youth, I caught a Greyhound coach up north with my high school buddies from The Group. We did Schoolies our way. We didn't spend it passed out in the mall vomiting up alcohol or in a hospital ward getting patched up after getting into a punch-up, as many inexperienced high school graduates did. Our group avoided the yobbo action taking place in the heart of the Gold Coast and stayed at a more subdued venue, a youth hostel at Coolangatta Beach.

We also waited until most of the less sophisticated, trashy high school students had come and gone. The Group arrived fashionably late in January 1991. During the daylight we hung out at the beach and had a blast doing kids' stuff, like visiting Sea World and taking a day trip to South Stradbroke Island. By night, we went on our first booze cruise and laughed at the tacky adults partaking in a wet T-shirt competition. They were all so tragic. We checked out dodgy heterosexual pick-up clubs, like The Tunnel. As usual, it didn't take long for my group of seasoned dance party veterans to become the centre of attention.

'What are you on?' a blond girl, yelled in my ear.

'Natural high!' I yelled.

'Liar!' The girl smiled with wide eyes. 'I'm Amanda. Who are you, sweetheart?'

'Nathan,' I said unenthusiastically.

'Nice to meet you, Nathan!' she said. 'Are you single?'

'Taken.' I nodded towards Anna's direction.

'Have fun!' she said before approaching another guy.

Even though more than one pretty girl approached me during Schoolies, nothing sexual happened. I knew I was 100% queer, as did my friends. I'd wasted no time coming out after we'd escaped high school. My friends accepted me for who I was but were also respectful I hadn't told my parents, so I was keeping my news secret, for now.

As I danced with Anna and Lee danced with Sarah, most other people in the club naturally assumed we were couples and taken. We made fun of the obvious desperados in the club, like the toolies, men in their twenties who migrated to the Gold Coast to pick-up HSC graduates, or anything that had a pulse on the dance floor. We came up with our own special code when we came across a toolie.

'Tu marido!' we'd cry with laughter. Sarah had taught us in Spanish this saying meant, *'Your husband!'* It was the ultimate insult and our little private in-joke to be used against the unsuspecting. That was, until Anna called an alarmingly hairy man who was dancing closer and closer to her, 'Tu marido!'

'Ah!' he protested. 'I'm not married!'

We burst into laughter when he held up his un-banded wedding ring finger in protest. Unfortunately, it became apparent the stranger was Spanish and unmarried.

'What are the odds?' Lee laughed hysterically with us.

'Anna he's definitely your tu marido!' Sarah laughed along.

After Schoolies, we returned to Sydney. I invited Anna, Lee, and Sarah to go clubbing on Oxford Street. I wanted to go to a new hotspot called DCM (Don't Cry Mama), which was getting rave reviews in the nightlife street press 3D Magazine. Since I had come out to my high school friends after the HSC, I was eager to get back into the gay scene. I desperately wanted a boyfriend, and to find love. That meant returning to Oxford Street.

I deliberately chose to invite my school friends to party, rather than phoning Tiffany. This is because I knew Tiffany would insist on blasting speed the second we reconnected. Or at a minimum, we'd be doing E. My desire to keep a clear head before starting university prevented me from reconnecting with Tiffany.

Dressed in all black, our group grew excited as we walked up the stairs to enter DCM. It was located on the opposite side of Oxford Street from the legendary Exchange Hotel. Once inside, it soon became obvious that Anna, Lee, and Sarah were no longer as comfortable hanging out on the gay scene as they'd been when we were impressionable sixteen-years olds, eager for a thrill and happy to walk on the wild side while off-our-faces.

Now sober, Anna especially had changed her tune. 'Not one straight man in sight!' she scoffed, unimpressed.

Sarah nodded in agreement. Their first reaction upon seeing the dance floor was filled with impossibly handsome looking men was that they didn't fit in. It was a crowd of gym-bodies with bare, muscular chests and perfect smiles.

'Just like always.' Lee grinned.

I nodded in agreement. I was in heaven, and wondered if I could catch the eye of a potential partner. The club was packed with the most beautiful people in Sydney. Not one ugly person had been allowed in. The beautiful people were dancing wildly to 'Move your body' by Xpansions. Green laser lights shot above the crowd. Then the beams suddenly focused on a man dancing on a podium. He was shirtless, tall, handsome and was a clearly overly confident young man who danced like he thought he was the club's main attraction. As he bounced above the crowd, some cheered him on.

'Go, Dom!' I heard someone yell over the music.

I couldn't keep my eyes off the boy they called Dom. With his large physique, he looked like an Aussie footballer. He was dripping with sweat, moving to the beat at an increasing speed, dancing like one of Madonna's back-up dancers. 'Do you think he's gay?' I asked Anna with a knowing grin.

'Of course. But he's out of your league!'

'Thanks a lot!' I was annoyed at how visibly tense Anna seemed at being inside a gay club now she was a young adult. I got the sense that the men dancing inside DCM were *over* the increasing number of straight people like

Anna coming to Oxford Street clubs and not having the common decency to contain looks of disappointment at the regulars. Like she or Sarah had a chance.

'Tourists!' hissed a handsome gay couple as they passed us, confirming my suspicions. The fashionable young queer couple giggled to each other before hitting the dance floor. It was at this moment that I realised that if I wanted to pick up on the gay scene, I'd have to do it alone.

That's how I found myself staring intensely at my reflection in the bathroom mirror in my parents' home the following night. I was trying to get my hair styled just right. I thought my hair had to be perfect to pick up or be picked up. Just as I'd done at the age of sixteen, I planned to go out to Oxford Street with the sole intention of hooking up with another a man. Hopefully, it would be one that looked like the attractive boy, Dom, dancing on the podium of DCM. At eighteen years old, he was the man I wanted to hook up with, a boy who looked like an Aussie football legend and danced like a pop star.

For my first solo young adult misadventure, I chose the bar with the most men hanging outside the entrance, The Albury Hotel. The Albury was an art deco bar on the corner of Oxford and Barcom Streets behind St Vincent's Hospital. In the centre of the bar was a long narrow display of top-shelf liqueurs being served by the finest male specimens the gay scene had to offer. The uniform of an Albury barman consisted of tight jeans, boots or sneakers, and that was it. The other requirement was having a muscular, tanned, waxed chest and stunning good looks. The Albury Hotel barmen glided behind the bar, serving patron after drooling patron until midnight. One of them was me. I stood in the bar surrounded by men feeling incredibly alone. I was unable to focus on any of the other patrons because I was too busy fantasising about what it would be like to go to bed with one of the impossibly perfect looking barmen.

All the men inside the packed bar seemed so untouchable. Instead of feeling like I was with my people, I felt like an outsider, like I was trying to break into a world that was completely sealed off by invisible warning tape.

With my skinny frame, I felt out of place. Undesirable. I wondered if it were me or the gay scene itself that was changing? The men standing inside the bar were more muscular than what had been fashionable in the 80s. Still being a skinny teenager, I felt like an undefined nothing compared to the beefy men cruising the gay bars of Oxford Street. Fortunately, a group of equally skinny boys just older than me noticed I was by myself.

'Waiting for someone?' a cute blue-eyed boy asked.

I nodded, pretending I wasn't alone.

'I'm Boyd,' the cute blue-eyed boy introduced himself.

'Nathan.' I smiled, relieved to be seen talking to someone. It was nice not having to lie about my real name anymore, as I'd previously done when I was younger, while in the closet and afraid of people discovering my secret self. 'Come here often, Boyd?' I asked.

'Honey, I practically live here.' Boyd grinned. 'But I haven't seen you here before. What's your story?'

'Hoping to meet Mr Right!' I grinned.

'Aren't we all!' Boyd smiled. 'Tell you where you'll meet him. At Sweat.'

'Sweat?'

'Tomorrow night. Alexandria stadium. It's the new Hordern. You got to be there!'

'For sure!' I smiled, having no idea where the Alexandria stadium was.

It was the first I'd heard about the party. Sweat had only been advertised in the gay press that I didn't read. I hoped there were still tickets on sale, especially when Boyd insisted that we meet again tomorrow night at The Albury to go to the party together.

That night, even though I went home alone, before I left, I scored a kiss and a hug from Boyd.

~

The Sweat party was the first gay dance party I attended with my new gay friend. After meeting up inside The Albury Hotel, I shared a taxi with Boyd to Alexandria stadium.

'Ready to party?' Boyd was dressed in tight-fitting neon blue bicycle shorts and a white singlet. It looked like he'd had already popped something, given how dilated his pupils were.

As the taxi pulled up outside Alexandria stadium, I could see why it was becoming the new preferred dance party venue. The music was booming, and there were no residents nearby to complain about it.

Together as we entered the stadium, I fondly felt like I was stepping back in time. The stadium had the same charged atmosphere as Club Hordern back in its glory days. The music was deafening, the lasers were blindingly intense, and the crowd's sweat heated the air inside. It was no coincidence the party was called Sweat. Not being on any illicit substances, I was able to experience the party sober and coherently.

'Maybe it isn't too late to score an E?' I said as Boyd held my hand and dragged me into the middle of the dance floor. On the packed dance floor, surrounded by athletic men, I appreciated how out of sync I had become with what was happening on the gay scene. Most men were bulging with muscles and wore practically nothing. Instead of dancing, it looked like they were flexing, as though they were competing at a Mr Universe competition. Everyone was watching and judging. No one seemed to mind it even a bit though.

By comparison, I'd naively dressed for such an event. I wore jeans and a grey T-shirt that I sweated through in no time. All the men surrounding us were dressed like Boyd, in gym gear and sweat-resistant materials designed to dance the night away like it was a marathon aerobics class. The experienced dance party queens wore spandex and little else to dance till dawn.

The only other man who was dressed simply, in a tightly fitted white Bonds t-shirt and light blue Levi jeans, was the prominent National Rugby League star player, Ian Roberts. I couldn't believe my eyes when I spotted Ian casually walking through the crowd.

'Tell me I'm not hallucinating!' Boyd yelled in my ear.

'No, you're not! I see him too. But I don't believe what I'm seeing!' I yelled with excitement.

Ian looked like a real-life vision of a Tom of Finland drawing come to life, a tall, rugged, naturally handsome man with bulging biceps, a giant defined chest, and a strong square angular jaw line. He had a serious expression on his face as he moved through the mass of half-naked bodies, everyone gawking at him. None of the other gym-bunnies and muscle queens on the dance floor could believe what they were seeing. Ian Roberts, one of the most handsome men from the NRL, the straightest sport in the country, was wandering through the gayest party in town.

'Do you think that straights are discovering how cool our dance parties are?' Boyd yelled in my ear. 'Or is Ian one of us?'

The idea that an Australian sportsman or woman who was at the top of their game could be gay was inconceivable in the early 90s. Our eyes didn't stray from the sight of Ian as he passed by, vanishing into the crowd of queer men and straight girls dancing relentlessly.

I was surprised to see that Ian had chosen to wear a similar outfit to the one I did. Only Ian had something extra that I now longed for, something I knew I desperately needed to become the desire for another man's attention: a perfect, gym-sculpted, athletic body.

Ian left a trail of dazed and lustful expressions as he made his way through the crowd. I desperately wished I could have a boyfriend who looked like that.

Other than the sighting of Ian Roberts, I found the experience of partying at the Alexandria stadium and not being on E a largely unsatisfying experience. This dance party only made me grateful I was leaving Sydney to concentrate on my future studies in a country town, away from the gay scene.

A week later, after saying goodbye to Mum and Dad, I watched endless gumtrees rush by the window of a Greyhound bus. I wondered if I was doing the right thing by leaving it all behind. Who decides to get away from the Sydney drug scene by moving to a town only an hour's drive from Australia's original hippy commune settlement in Nimbin?

BUDDIES WITH BENEFITS

I 'D TAKEN A leap of faith with my decision to move to Lismore, a country town I knew nothing about, a place where I had no friends or family. However, that was the point: to make a new start. While I'd told my closest schoolfriends I was gay, I wasn't ready to admit it to my parents, my loving parents who were paying my living-away-from-home expenses.

Riding on the coach to Lismore was exciting, but I also felt claustrophobic, trapped inside the bus bound for my new temporary home. The only thing keeping me sane was the cassette tape I'd used to record music off the radio. On my Walkman, I listened to music that reminded me of my misspent youth. Electribe 101's lead singer Billie Ray Martin singing 'Talking with myself' conjured happy nights spent disorientated on the dance floor.

I was feeling disorientated about the future. Finally, I would be on my own for the very first time. I would have to find a new group of friends. Maybe this time, I could be honest about who I was from the start, let people know from day one that I was gay. I contemplated what that would be like.

Imagine, no more feeling the need to pretend I was heterosexual to fit in and avoid people judging me for being a faggot. Heterosexual was something I still pretended to be for my parents. Without their support, I'd be screwed, possibly homeless. Forget about being cut off emotionally, I was a practical young man when it came to finances. Admittedly, I hadn't so much as come out as peeked outside the closet door, told my best friends not to tell anyone, and then crept back in the security of the closet.

Not that there was much to tell. It wasn't like I was a practicing gay man. Since putting partying on pause to complete the HSC, I hadn't been with another man. I had gone to my high school formal with a girl, Anna. For all appearances' sake, I was a raving hetero. It wasn't like I had been brave enough to take a boy to my high school formal. In 1990 that was unthinkable. We would have been killed, or, at a minimum, potentially beaten up.

Feeling crusty from a 10-hour bus trip, I was pleasantly surprised at how fresh and earthy the air of Lismore smelt compared to Sydney. The rolling green hills and tall trees of the Northern Rivers area made me feel alive and recharged as I embarked on the next part of the journey, meeting the university dorm assignment coordinator.

The dorms were in Lismore Heights, perched high above the town, looking down on the university campus in the valley below. I was assigned to a room in a three-bedroom unit. To my relief, my roommates were two girls: an Asian exchange student and a girl from Queensland who was going to study sports science.

After unpacking my bags, the first thing I did was stick photographs of myself with my dearest friends on the brick wall. I smiled at a photo in which my arms were locked around my mates. I was proud of the printed photographs. It was evidence of how much me and my friends loved each other and how cool we were. One of the pictures was taken the night we went to our first FUN Love party, the night we tried ecstasy for the first time. The group photos made me feel less on my own as I prepared for my first lecture. It was time to build a new group of friends.

Lining up outside an unfamiliar lecture room with a bunch of complete strangers was a daunting experience. I listened to people make small talk.

'Where are you from?'

'Which school did you go to?'

'Why did you pick this course?'

As I waited, I was excited to check out my new classmates, eager to see what the competition was like among the BA Media Communication class of 1991.

I was entertaining the notion of becoming a journalist, or an author.

Like most Generation X kids, I was motivated by materialism, having enjoyed a consumer-driven upbringing. The idea of making a living that wasn't going to pay well was unpalatable. I needed to secure a job that would earn big bucks, and fast!

This was why I chose a BA in Media Communication. I foolishly believed that, as a journalist, I'd have a chance at earning the dollars. I didn't realise this only happened for the lucky few who read the evening news and advertisements disguised as current affairs. Because I considered myself to have the right look, with a deep voice and dark newsreader hair — the type of look fit to be seen on TV — I was certain this would be my destiny. My career aspiration became another reason that made me think twice about coming out publicly. I knew I would have to stay in the closet professionally to have a shot at a career in media.

That's what most gay people in the entertainment industry did. Just look at Rock Hudson, for example. The only thing that made him come out was when it was revealed he had contracted HIV and developed AIDS. No one on TV was brave enough to be openly gay in the early 1990s.

I began to wonder if anyone else waiting outside the lecture room was also in the closet? Especially as there were several very good-looking men waiting outside. That was the first thing that caught my eye as I sized up the competition, the fine assortment of surfer dudes who had also gravitated to Lismore to 'study'.

'What's your name?' a guy with piercing ocean blue eyes, shaggy blond hair, and a deep tan asked me.

I was taken back by how handsome this stranger was. 'Nathan,' I said after momentarily forgetting what my real name was. 'What's yours?'

'Matt,' the broad-shouldered boy answered in a deep tone.

He'd make the perfect news presenter, I thought to myself. I struggled to focus on the getting-to-know-you small talk. 'Where are you from, Matt?'

'Sydney. Same as you, right?'

'How could you tell?'

'You don't look like a local Buddie.' Matt grinned as the students were let into the lecture room.

For some unknown reason, I took a seat that looked safe next to one of the prettiest girls in the room. She was dressed like a 1940s-film star, wearing a vintage floral cotton dress. She made it look edgy by wearing cherry Doc Martin boots. Her medium length hair was dyed red and blow-dried into a bob that curled inward to frame her smiling face.

'Hello. I'm Claire.' The girl smiled at me politely.

'Nathan.' I smiled back.

'You're not a local, are you?'

'How can everyone tell?'

'You look like a big city slicker, mister!' Claire was all giggles. She was doing the same as I was, checking out the available male talent in the lecture room. She'd looked thrilled when I'd sat next to her.

I wondered what it was about me that screamed that I was an outsider. I didn't realise that it was because I was the only boy in the class who had gelled his hair like James Dean, wore black Doc Martin boots, and rolled up the bottom of my 501 Levi's jeans along with the sleeves of my white Bonds t-shirt. I thought it was cool to dress like I was ready to appear on the set of The Wild Ones. I wasn't like the rest of the boys in class who wore board shorts and thongs in anticipation of heading to Byron Bay the minute classes were over, one of which was Matt.

I was thrilled when Matt chose to take the empty seat next to me. At university, the seats were chairs combined with a desktop into one unit. We were moving up in the world. I smiled, excited by Matt's mere presence, but then Matt moved in to say something under his breath.

'Who's the babe next to you?'

In that instant, I froze. I suddenly knew there was no way I was going to be openly gay in my new life away from home. I just couldn't do it. I wasn't brave enough. It was easier to pretend I was like Matt, just one of the straight fellas.

'I saw her first,' I whispered back to Matt, to which Matt nodded in an unspoken agreement. He spent the rest of the class checking out the other girls in the room.

After our first class, I invited Claire and Matt to grab a coffee before the next lecture.

In the university café, Matt admitted the main reason he'd chosen to study in Lismore was because it was located so close to Byron Bay. 'It's the sickest beach in NSW,' Matt said as he blew smoke from a hand-rolled cigarette. 'Plus, there's a steady supply of high-quality dope in this neck of the woods.'

'What more could you want from an education?' Claire said sarcastically with a smile as she gave me a look that was filled with disapproval.

I grinned but said nothing judgmental. I appreciated Matt's reasoning. There wasn't a thing Matt could have said that I didn't like.

Claire admitted, 'I just wanted to escape from my parents' home and living in Tamworth. That's why I came to Lismore.'

'Me too!' I exclaimed, excited to make a connection. 'I had to escape my parents and Sydney.'

'Really? I had no issues with my folks,' Matt said. 'Mind you, it wasn't always a smooth ride having a conservative politician for a father.'

'You're dad's a conservative politician?' Claire seemed impressed. Matt nodded, yes. 'Didn't that kind of fuck you up?' Claire blurted out.

'Not at all,' Matt shrugged and blew a cloud of smoke. 'Not in the slightest.'

Matt drove a black convertible jeep his father had bought him as an 18th birthday present. In the coming days, Matt was more than happy to pick Claire and I up from the dorms to drive to our lectures. With each road trip to class, I couldn't work out why Matt constantly blasted Madonna's Immaculate Collection CD, especially the dance mix of 'Like a Prayer'. Was it because he came from a super religious family? Or was it because he was into songs from the most famous gay icon of all time for other reasons. I hoped it was for other reasons.

Each day, I tried hard to conceal the crush I was developing for Matt as I rode in the passenger seat. I had to catch myself from sneaking peeks at Matt's muscular, tanned hairy legs, a split-second before Matt caught me looking.

Claire sat behind Matt and me in the back seat. She occasionally stretched her arms freely in the air to feel the wind rush between her fingers. Claire was oblivious to the deep attraction I was developing for the boy behind the wheel.

In my first few weeks of getting settled into campus life, I learnt all about the benefits of studying in the Northern Rivers area. Through Matt, I discovered first-hand how Lismore was a convenient half hour drive away from the beachside town of Byron Bay. It was a popular retreat for new age hippies and real ones that had survived the 60s and 70s who were still wandering the streets with their hair in dreadlocks and wearing tie-died clothes. They all knew someone who was selling organically grown marijuana. The combination of the university's unique location and my new friendship with a stunning, tall, blond surfer boy was all it took for me to wrap my lips around a bong packed with marijuana.

As the dirty bong water bubbled, I learnt that I couldn't escape drugs by leaving the city. No matter where you went in Australia, drugs were everywhere. By studying away from the Sydney, I'd succeeded in escaping the dance party scene, but not drugs.

Getting stoned became an after-class ritual.

At the end of the first week of university lectures, I sat with Matt in my dorm bedroom talking about our assignments and enjoying our third or fourth cone.

Matt put on a tape of The Stone Roses album, playing 'I wanna be adored' as he opened up to reveal he'd just broken up with his girlfriend, Kelly. Soon, we listened to 'Fools gold' while passing the bong back and forth.

'Kelly's a gorgeous ballet dancer with a smoking hot body.' Matt sucked on the bong, the water bubbled, and then he blew a thick plume of smoke into the room. 'I'm still getting over her. Do you have a girlfriend?'

'No,' I said blankly. 'Not at the moment.'

'What do you think about Claire?'

'She's sweet.'

'She sure is…' After admitting this, Matt said something that took my utterly stoned brain off-guard. 'Fuck, I'm horny.' Matt leaned back on my single bed.

My heart skipped a beat. The shape of Matt's erection was sticking up beneath his Billabong board shorts. It was unmissable. I felt intense emotions at the sight of Matt in my dorm room with a hard-on. Immediately, my dick grew uncomfortably hard. Suddenly, my jeans felt too tight.

Neither of us said anything for a few seconds. We made blood-shot eye contact. My eyes wandered back to Matt's crotch. Neither of us said anything for a few more seconds until Matt broke the silence. 'Want to suck my dick?' His tone was nonchalant. Distant, yet, inviting. 'I'm so fuckin' stoned right now. Man, I have no clue what I'm saying.'

'Yeah. Me too man.' I tried to match Matt's nonchalant tone and continued to pretend I was straight as I took a leap of faith. I reached over to pull loose the drawstring of Matt's board shorts.

Matt closed his eyes.

It had been ages since I'd had been with another man. Holding the rock-hard dick of another supposedly heterosexual boy completely blew my numb mind. I wasn't sure this series of events would have happened so naturally if Matt knew that I was gay.

This was my first memorable lesson at university, how a supposedly heterosexual guy was cool about getting off with another supposedly heterosexual guy when in an altered state. We weren't gay, just two horny mates who'd had too many cones of locally grown weed.

It must have been because of the Nimbin weed.

WEIRD COUPLE

WHILE WAITING FOR the lecturer to show for a tutorial on journalism, I came to realise there were two openly gay guys in my class. One was a very handsome boy named Brad. Brad didn't have to announce he was gay for me to know his sexual orientation. I could tell just by the way Brad spoke, what he wore, and how confidently he acted. He was extremely flamboyant and got along with strangers so effortlessly, it seemed. Brad was the vision of perfection.

Brad and I had similar physiques. But what set Brad and I apart was that Brad was seriously good looking, in a Hollywood, leading man kind of way. However, I didn't find Brad nearly as appealing as I did the more rugged and heterosexual-acting Matt.

Brad was a little older than me. He was twenty-one years old. He'd also grown up in Sydney, but had lived on the other side of the bridge, in Manly. After high school, he'd told everyone waiting that he was backpacking overseas until he ran out of money. Brad decided to study in Lismore because of its bohemian lifestyle.

The other openly gay guy in our class was an older man named John.

'How old are you, John?' Claire asked politely, a question, we had all been thinking.

'Thirty-eight,' John replied confidently and with a chuckle.

'Seriously?' Brad exclaimed.

'You don't look thirty-eight at all!' I complimented John.

'Yeah,' Matt agreed. 'Aren't people your age meant to have grey hair?'

'That doesn't happen to gay people. God figures we've been through enough shit already.' John laughed intensely at his own joke as we studied his face to assess if he'd had any work done. Until hearing John's remark, I'd had no idea he was gay. John didn't fit my perception of what a gay guy looked or acted like. University taught me another important lesson: gay people came in all shapes, sizes, and ages.

Apart from Matt, it was the mature age student John that my eyes wandered to when I grew bored and daydreamed in class. It didn't matter to me that John was twice my age. I just couldn't stop my eyes from gravitating towards his upper body. He'd missed his calling as an Albury bar man. Maybe he had been one when he was younger, I wondered. I decided I'd ask John if he'd ever worked there. When I finally did during the journalism tutorial, John had the biggest smile.

'Aren't you a sweetheart!' John grinned. 'No, I was something far more mundane before moving up to the Northern Rivers. I was an accountant."

When my eyes weren't sneaking glances of Matt's thighs while driving to university, my eyes wandered to the outline of John's chest under his Ralph Lauren polo tops. Thoughts of sexual activity and fantasies with these two males frequently interrupted my concentration and made learning about the Australian media landscape difficult. I was eighteen years old and my hormones were racing. My attraction to John surprised me, mainly because John didn't wear fashionable clothes. He didn't have an impeccable sense of style that came naturally to most gay men. I thought John's choice of clothes were out of date. This is why it confused me how much I got turned on by checking out John. Especially since there was something that turned me off John: his over-bearing laugh.

Whenever John tried to be funny, he'd laugh loudly at his own jokes, even when no one else laughed or found them amusing. It didn't take long before the whole class gave each other eyerolls, unbeknownst to John, whenever he made one of his unfunny jokes. Despite the generation gap, I still found something oddly appealing about John.

Regardless of making new out-and-proud friends like Brad and John, I couldn't shake the pressure to pretend to be straight and remained in the closet. That's probably why Claire and I became fast friends. She was not just a friend, but also a cover. We were more like girlfriends that sat together in every lecture, drank coffee, and smoked joints after class. We went for walks in the small pocket of rain forest reserve near our dorms. Claire and I soon shared cassette tapes of The Smiths, Depeche Mode, and The Cure. But the one thing Claire couldn't stand about me was my 'commercial' taste in music. She laughed when I tried to share Madonna's first self-titled album. Claire thought Madonna was 'smelly'. She didn't read my commercial musical taste as a clue I was homosexual.

On weekends, Brad, Claire, and I loved being passengers in Matt's convertible as we cruised through the green scenic hills of Bangalow. Matt drove us up to the Byron Bay lighthouse instead of us reading prescribed textbooks. We watched the sunset over the horizon.

Brad couldn't believe it when he found out Matt's father was a conservative politician.

'For real?' Brad laughed, as he passed a joint back to Matt.

'Minister Adler,' Matt admitted as smoke spilled from his grin.

'Did that make things difficult for you growing up in such a right-wing environment?' Brad asked thoughtfully.

'Not at all,' Matt answered in all seriousness. 'Dad is a pillar of our community; he gave me a good moral compass.' After Matt said this, I wondered if that 'moral compass' directed Matt towards letting other boys go down south on his dick when he got stoned?

Since Brad, Claire, Matt, and I became a friendly foursome, I never found myself in a situation with Matt where we were alone and stoned again. I desperately hoped what once had happened between us wouldn't be a one-off incident, just a case of boys being boys. I also hoped that Matt hadn't switched his secret sexual attention to Brad. After all, Brad was much better looking. Also, there was Claire. Matt was infatuated with her beauty. Each time she spoke, he smiled like a love-sick schoolboy.

However, Claire only had eyes for me. By the middle of the first semester, it was obvious a love triangle had established between me and Matt for Claire's attention.

After working late into the evening on a journalism assignment, Claire asked if she could stay over in my dorm room. 'It's so late.' Claire smiled. 'Do you mind if I stay here tonight?'

'Um…' I wasn't sure of how to avoid answering this question without seeming fruity. At the same time, I was worried where this request might lead.

'I get scared walking in the dark back to my dorm this time of night,' Claire pleaded.

'Okay.' I smiled while secretly dreading where this was going to lead. I didn't put up a fight and invited Claire to sleep with me in my single dorm bed. Within minutes of switching off the lights, Claire cuddled up and began kissing my lips gently as her hand moved across my fine chest hair. For some reason, I played along and didn't protest when Claire pulled off her top and bra. Although it did alarm me seeing the sight of my friend's perky breasts.

I had no idea what I was meant to do next. Both our hearts were racing for very different reasons. It all happened so fast and it felt so unnatural to feel a girl's breasts. In some way, I hoped it would arouse me. But I felt nothing. It just reinforced how truly gay I really was. However, this simply didn't feel like the right time to come out to my new best friend. Despite my conflicted feelings, Claire was still in for a surprise. When she felt my penis under my pyjama shorts, she exclaimed, 'You're hard!'

It had been so long since I'd had my last sexual contact with Matt that my body was reacting to the slightest bit of attention. My hormones betrayed me and made me appear straight and an easy target for another's affection. While I was hard between the legs, inside I was desperately uncomfortable and wished two things: one, that it was Matt this was happening with, and two, that I was straight, so I wouldn't feel like such a fraud.

Feeling Claire's breasts as she touched my cock was as far as I was prepared to go before I announced, 'Man, I'm tired. Let's get some shut eye.'

'Oh,' Claire sounded confused. 'Okay!' Claire took her hand off my crotch and rested it back on my chest as we settled into each other's arms. 'It's nice to be held,' Claire whispered.

'You're so soft,' I whispered back hoping this was the right thing to say. I wondered, why couldn't this happen with another man? At eighteen-years-old, what I wanted most was to be in a loving relationship with another guy my own age, to have a boyfriend. That's all I wanted.

I pretended Matt was in my arms. I made believe it was Matt I'd been kissing before drifting off to sleep.

~

The next morning, Claire communicated to everyone in the Communication course that we were officially an item. She did so by holding my hand and announced to Brad and Matt that we'd spent the night together. 'It finally happened!' Claire grinned.

'So, you guys are a thing?' Brad's handsome jaw dropped. He looked slightly amused. 'How did that happen?'

'It just happened!' I responded perhaps too defensively.

'That's awesome,' Matt said without any enthusiasm and stared at me with what looked like an angry expression.

~

The next morning, Matt didn't show as usual to pick up Claire and I to drive to university.

'Where do you think he is?' Claire asked after we waited for more than twenty minutes for Matt's black convertible to show. This was unusual.

'Maybe he's not feeling well?' I offered, but had an uneasy feeling there was another reason why Matt was a no show. I wasn't sure whether Matt was jealous of Claire or me. Deep down, I hoped it was of me. But I suspected it was more for Claire.

After walking from our dorms down the track of the steep hill to our university campus, we turned up to class. Matt was sitting in the back row and avoided eye contact with us.

'He just totally ignored me!' Claire exclaimed with her eyes glued on Matt.

Matt pretended he had no idea Claire was staring at him. Then he totally ignored me when I waved to him. I felt uneasy. In the coming weeks, Matt sat only with the other stoner surfer dudes at the back of the class. Brad overheard some boys during class saying they thought Claire and I were a 'weird couple'.

PREFERS BOYS

CLAIRE AND I were a happy couple that only kissed and hugged. That was as far as I was prepared to go sexually with a girl. As boyfriend and girlfriend, we felt something close to love. But we both knew something was strange about our romance.

During the first few weeks of dating, I noticed unusual things about my girlfriend. It had nothing to do with the fact that Claire identified herself as an outsider to mainstream society. She told me she hated the experience of growing up in the conventional country town of Tamworth. Claire always felt like the odd one out, a feminist, an aspiring artist, and a naturalist who drank chamomile tea when she had cramps from period pain. Claire said she wasn't like the rest of the girls in Tamworth. These were aspects of her personality that made her fellow high school classmates and her very own relatives brand her a weirdo. Claire's small group of high school friends had also been misfits. Unlike my group of misfit multicultural friends who had grown up in the big city, none of the kids in Claire's country town thought Claire's friends were cool. They had been bullied remorselessly.

'We developed thick skins.' Claire shrugged off the obviously painful experiences of her adolescence.

While I liked Claire's rebellious attitude, there was something about her that started to unnerve me. She didn't eat much. She didn't eat much at all. I couldn't help noticing that Claire appeared to be getting thinner in the short time I knew her. What was even more alarming was that when Claire did eat, she always headed immediately for the bathroom. She was so fixated on getting to the toilet within minutes of eating that nothing else mattered. It was like she went into a trance.

I started to suspect she might be anorexic or bulimic or both. Either way, she was a complicated girl. But I didn't know how to bring up this observation, especially as I began to suspect that Claire had her own suspicions about me being a bit unusual. After having no real sexual activity since we started dating, I could tell Claire had started to think I was hiding a secret of my own.

Out of the blue, Claire asked, 'How many girlfriends have you had previously?' Claire had made it into university because she was super smart. She followed that question up with, 'Is there someone special back home?'

The suspicion of me being gay and Claire having an eating disorder was something neither of us was willing to discuss. That lasted until a chilly evening watching a disturbing episode of David Lynch's 'Twin Peaks' with Brad in my dorm. It was just past nine o'clock and Claire had drifted off in my arms.

Suddenly, Claire disturbed the entire university dorm residence with a blood-curdling scream. Before the scream had erupted, we'd heard Claire mumble gurgled words. 'No. Don't go there… Help me… Help!' When she woke, Claire was completely unaware of where she was and what she'd been saying. Once again, she seemed to be in a trance-like state.

'Are you, okay?' I held Claire by her shoulders and looked directly into her bloodshot eyes. For a moment, it seemed like she was a different person.

Gradually, she reconnected with reality, and her face flushed red. 'I'm so embarrassed! I don't know what happened.' Claire let out a shaky breath.

'You were having a bad dream!' Brad rubbed Claire's arm to comfort her.

'It was so scary.' Claire paused as she struggled to recollect the nightmare. 'There was a giant farm tractor with big claws trying to get me.'

Brad and I shared a quick look, confirming we both agreed how strange this incident was. Suddenly, it felt like we were living inside an episode of Twin Peaks.

～○

Strange became the norm with Claire. Her beautiful vintage dresses hung off her gaunt frame. The bones in her wrists were becoming increasingly visible under her pale skin. I knew Claire needed to seek help when she had another nightmarish outburst, only more publicly.

In our Public Relations lecture, Claire gave the entire class of forty students the scoop of a lifetime regarding how unbalanced she was from not eating and not sleeping properly.

'Noooo!' Claire yelled out of nowhere. The entire class jumped. When Claire woke, she looked horrified. Realising where she was, Claire panicked and ran out of the lecture room in tears. Our lecturer, Sonya Wong, ran after Claire and brought her back to class in a caring and concerned manner. Claire looked like a lost little girl as she tearfully collected her belongings and left the room.

The class was left feeling rattled and confused by what just happened, exchanging concerned looks for Claire, one of which I caught from Matt. He looked genuinely concerned and mouthed the words to me, *'What the fuck?'* It was the first thing he'd said to me since ignoring me because I'd started dating Claire.

Unfortunately, I had no answer for what just took place. I shook my head, unsure in response to Matt's confused expression.

During the lunch break, I hurried up the forest track to the university dorms in Lismore Heights. I found Claire in her room. She had calmed down and was sipping chamomile tea, but she still looked shaken.

'I'm so utterly embarrassed.' She laughed nervously. Her eyes were red, puffy and teary.

'What's wrong?' I asked, determined to get to the bottom of what was going on.

'I –,' Claire sounded lost. 'I don't know. I can't remember.'

As Claire spoke, I got the feeling I was not speaking with the eighteen-year-old young woman. Claire sounded more like a frightened girl. I was deeply concerned about her welfare. I had already lost one very close friend to mental illness, Evelyn, who had been diagnosed at sixteen of being schizophrenic. I couldn't bear the thought of something similar happening to another person.

'Claire, please don't take this the wrong way,' I spoke softly and chose my words carefully. 'I think you need help.'

Claire said sarcastically and with dark amusement, 'Help?'

'Yes, help,' I said with complete sincerity. 'I had a friend who went through something like this.' It took an hour to convince my frightened girlfriend to take my hand and come with me to see a university counsellor. Upon seeing the way that Claire was being led into the waiting room and how disconnected she appeared, the receptionist recognised an emergency case and ushered Claire in to see the next available counsellor.

As the door closed behind her, I let out a giant sigh of relief. The day's events left me feeling extremely stressed-out. Not for the first time, I seriously wondered if pretending to be straight was worth it. For the sake of appearances, I was in a romantic relationship with the prettiest and apparently most mentally unstable girlfriend to date. I was seriously starting to consider the possibility that having a girlfriend wasn't something I was meant to have. Perhaps the recent events with Claire were a sign from the universe; it was time to stop pretending to be heterosexual.

I should never have hooked up with a girl who was the love interest of the boy I had a crush on. It was all too complicated. I had to end this romantic relationship. I regretted my inability to find the courage to be openly gay like Brad and John. If I'd been honest about who I really was with my new university classmates from day one, I wouldn't be caught up in this complicated charade. I wouldn't be lying about my sexuality to a girl who had enough emotional and psychological problems to deal with, let alone finding out her boyfriend also prefers boys.

I knew I'd have to be very careful how I handled the situation once Claire came out of her counselling session. I didn't want to break up and be the one to push her over the edge. I suddenly felt like I needed to see a counsellor of my own to deal with what was running through my mind. I was staying in the closet to maintain appearances, had a mentally ill girlfriend, and had a secret crush on a straight-acting young man. My plan to avoid distractions at university was a flawed plan and I had and no idea what to do next. I had to talk to someone. My heart and mind were racing. As Claire faced her demons in the university counsellor's office, I was finally ready to face my own. I searched the campus to find the one person I thought would understand: Brad.

I checked the library, then the Mac labs, and rang Brad's home phone number but there was no answer. Brad was nowhere to be seen. Maybe he was with Matt! My heart sank at the very thought of it. After half an hour of looking, I spotted John sitting by himself reading in the campus courtyard. I approached him, hoping that someone more mature and experienced at being openly gay could be just what I needed.

'Can I talk to you?' I interrupted John from the book he had been reading.

'Sure,' John sounded surprised. 'Is Claire, okay?'

'She's seeing a counsellor right now. Can we go somewhere private? I really need to talk.'

'I know the perfect spot for a chat. There's a place just off campus.'

I followed John to the parking lot and jumped into his ute. My heart pounded as John drove me to a house on one of the mountains that overlooked the university campus.

John pulled up on a gravel driveway outside an old Queenslander style weatherboard, free standing house with an expansive front porch. 'Welcome to the Homestead!' He smiled, switching the engine off.

'The Homestead?' I wondered if this was John's home.

'The Homestead is something of an institution in this neck of the woods.' John laughed at his own comment. 'It's a safe house, or refuge, for gays and lesbians. It's part of a charity organisation. It's owned by a close friend, Michael. Come on.'

'How close? Is he your boyfriend?'

'No, he's just a friend!'

After we got out of the ute, I was introduced to the owner of The Homestead, who greeted John with a hug and a kiss. He told me it was a pleasure to meet me.

Michael had a grey beard and wore a bright tie-dyed top. 'Would you gentlemen like some herbal tea?' Michael was very chilled, welcoming, and relaxed.

'No, thanks,' John declined the offer.

'How about a joint?' Michael raised his brow suggestively, looking me directly in the eye.

John glanced at me to gauge my reaction.

'Yes, please! It's been a rough day!' I sounded stressed.

A minute after sharing one of the strongest joints I'd ever put my lips on, Michael intuitively knew that John and I needed some space to talk. He led us to a bench on the front porch. 'Seems like you boys have something heavy going on!' Michael commented before leaving us alone.

'What is it you want to talk about, Nathan?' John looked intrigued.

'I want to tell you something.' I took a deep breath. Even though I was incredibly stoned, I felt increasingly anxious about what I needed to admit.

'Okay,' John smiled warmly. He was wearing black-framed, Clark Kent-style reading glasses, as if he had x-ray vision. My superman re-adjusted his glasses to take a better look at me. Like he could see through my soul.

'I'm gay!' I let out a shaky breath. There, I said it!

John nodded. 'I suspected as much. Is that why Claire freaked out?'

'No!' I almost laughed as I felt increasingly flat and heavy from the joint. 'Claire's got her own problems. John, no one here knows about me being gay. Except you.'

'Nathan, I already assumed you were in the closet. Your voice, your body language, and your hair alone screams that you're queer. You're a per-fectionist in every sense. I guessed you were like me. Don't worry; it's fine. Being gay has its perks; trust me. I know coming out is a big deal. But believe me, it's for the best, and it does get better. Being openly gay rocks!' John laughed intensely.

As John spoke, I felt my body behave inappropriately. I was here to talk about coming out with someone who was more experienced at being openly gay than me. My intention had been to find out how people reacted when John had come out. Instead, I could feel my dick growing hard against my Levi jeans at the sight of John's defined chest underneath his Polo top.

John, an observant gay man, couldn't help but notice my bulging crotch. I didn't know if it was the dope or the roller-coaster ride of emotions, but I was suddenly horny as hell. Reading my body language and eye movements, John leaned in to kiss me on the lips. The next thing I knew, John and I were rubbing each other's crotches. Forbidden excitement and desire shot through my veins just for a few heated moments before we both paused to look at each other and burst into laughter.

'Well, that was unexpected!' John smirked, then laughed very intensely.

'Told you I was gay!' I laughed.

I never imagined coming out could be so sexually charged, especially with someone as mature as John was compared to me. This is how my third sexual relationship started with a fellow student. I was working my way through the student faculty, and it was only the first half of my first semester.

John became my secret relationship. I'd come out to him and then insisted he re-enter the closet with me. Mainly because I couldn't believe I was interested in a man twice my own age. I was afraid how the other students would react, especially Claire and Matt.

Also, little did I know, John had his own personal situation to consider. 'I don't know how my partner, Andy, is going to feel about this,' John revealed on the drive back to campus.

'You have a partner?'

TROPICAL FRUITS

I N THE WEEKS following her public breakdown, Claire received regular counselling sessions. She was referred to a local psychiatrist and prescribed mood stabilisers.

'The medication has stopped me from being a night owl,' Claire confided to me after class. 'It's ruining my ability to write through the night. That's what made me an artist. I barely know who I am now!'

'Does it make you feel any better?'

'Well, it has stopped the nightmares.'

'You'll have to give me some to try.'

'Do you have nightmares too?'

'Sometimes, I have dreams about drowning in pools of water.'

'Do you know why?'

'Yes.'

Claire's expression slowly turned serious. 'I haven't had the chance to thank you for convincing me to see the counsellor.' Claire took my hand in hers and gave it a squeeze. 'Thank you. You did the right thing.'

'I'm glad you're feeling better. Even if you're not burning the midnight oil anymore.' I put my arm around Claires shoulder.

Before we parted for the evening, I decided that, since Claire seemed okay mentally and was being so honest about what she was going through, it was time for me to share something. 'Claire, I have something that I want to tell you. Something I've wanted to say for a long time. Only I'm not sure how you're going to feel about it.'

'What is it?' Claire looked concerned in response to the gravity of my tone.

'I'm gay.' I hoped the mood stabilisers would soften the blow of this revelation.

'I knew it.' Claire's mouth extended to a knowing smile. 'The first night we went to bed together and you didn't go all the way, I thought to myself, I bet he's gay.'

'Why didn't you say something?'

'Right, I was meant to say you didn't make love with me, therefore you're gay! That would have made me sound a bit pretentious!'

'You're far from pretentious, Claire.' I gave my most recent and probably the last ex-girlfriend I'd ever have a loving hug. Our friendship reached a new level of closeness. Claire responded by holding on tight. I let her hold on, glad my news didn't upset her. Or, more importantly, that Claire didn't reject me as a friend. If anything, it sounded like she'd had a hunch about me.

On a drive through the scenic farm fields surrounding the township of Bangalow, I told John how Claire was relieved to hear that I was gay. That's what made John not so gently suggest I face up to the reality that I was always going to be gay.

'It's not a cold,' John said as he took a turn into a small village where we planned to have a secret lunch. 'It doesn't go away after a few days. You're always going to be this way'

I smiled. I felt safe with John. When we were alone together, I felt at peace. John's advice inspired me to come clean with all my university friends. I started with Brad over coffee in the university café.

'I knew all along,' Brad grinned. 'That's why I was so shocked you hooked up with Claire. Seemed kind of desperate to me.'

'How did you know?' I asked.

'Call it gay man's intuition.' Brad rolled his eyes. 'Sweetheart, it was so obvious! Anyway, now that you're officially an out and proud gay boy, we should go clubbing together on Oxford Street when we're in Sydney during the semester break.'

'I'd like that so much!' I told Brad. 'Maybe you can help me find a proper boyfriend!' I said with excitement.

'You never know your luck in the big city.' Brad flashed a smile.

I decided to tell Matt the same day, to hopefully repair our once very close friendship, crossing my fingers that Matt might reciprocate with the same revelation. That he'd become my first official boyfriend. Boy was I in for another surprise.

'No, you're not!' These were the first words out of Matt's mouth to the news.

'Yeah, seriously, I am. I've known since I was fifteen years old,' I admitted awkwardly. 'I've only just come to realise that being gay is what makes me – me. That's why I wanted you to be one of the first to know!'

'Shit, man, I thought you were like me!' Matt shrugged and looked concerned. 'You better not tell anyone about what we did, or I'll kill you. I swear, I'll kill you! Got that? I'll ruin you if you tarnish my dad's reputation!'

I backed away uneasy.

The look on Matt's once handsome face was contorted with hate and disgust, but mostly fear.

'You have nothing to worry about,' I told Matt and walked away deeply disturbed. The crush I once had on Matt shattered from hatred. My attraction was replaced with repulsion and a very uneasy feeling. I'd had sex with a right-wing homophobe.

⁓

John invited me to a broadcast called, 'Out FM with the Tropical Fruits'. He recorded the program at the university community radio station. I was excited as this was my first time in a real-life functioning studio. My eyes studied the walls covered with grey soundproof foam, microphones, CD players, and turntables. I grinned as John announced that tickets were on sale at the usual places, such as the local ACON Centre, for an upcoming dance party called, 'The Tropical Fruits Dance Spectacular'. Afterwards, John played 'It's raining men' by The Weather Girls, a song I hadn't heard in ages, but which I loved when I was a kid. Now I knew exactly why it had appealed to me at such an early age.

I sat silently in the background, learning what it was like to be an out and proud DJ. I watched with interest as John flicked switches like a pro to keep the show running smoothly single-handedly.

'How long have you been doing this?' I asked when John was off-air.

'Just over a year now. Started a few months after my partner, Andy, and I moved to Bangalow.'

'Why did you guys decide to move to the Northern Rivers?'

'It was to get away from the gay ghetto.' John seemed very serious. 'Andy and I decided we needed a tree-change. We both wanted to lead a more positive lifestyle than what we were used to in Newtown. The real catalyst was because my partner Andy contracted HIV.'

I was startled and caught off guard when John revealed this. Even though I'd partied on the gay scene of Oxford Street and done dance parties at The Hordern Pavilion, I was just young enough to somehow avoid the AIDS epidemic. I was deeply aware of how much the disease was affecting the queer community from education in high school. 'Are you HIV positive too?' I asked naively.

'No. I'm negative. Andy and I have had an open relationship for years now, but we always practiced safe sex. I guess that's why I'm clean.'

This blew my eighteen-year-old mind. I'd never met anyone who had HIV. Plus, I didn't even know what an *open relationship* was. As John went back on air to announce details for the upcoming fundraising dinner for the local ACON Centre, my mind was filled with questions about how John's partner contracted HIV. Had John ever been scared that he could catch HIV? I had been taught in sex education class at Dover Heights High school that the HIV virus couldn't be transmitted by saliva (and to always use a condom). I was still paranoid that I could have been exposed to the virus simply by kissing John recently. I felt guilty and stupid for even thinking it, but couldn't ignore the fear spreading irrationally in my mind. Having grown up in the 80s left me with a fear of AIDS.

As a pre-teen kid, I'd seen TV advertisement nightly that featured the Grim Reaper at a bowling alley knocking over all sorts of people, including a baby, to warn viewers about the deadly disease. It had left a vivid imprint on my young and impressionable mind. Also, it had triggered high school bullying and taunts accusing me of being a faggot going to die of AIDS. Worse still was when I started high school and all the kids called me Rock, after Rock Hudson who'd passed away from AIDS.

After John put the next track on air, Gloria Gaynor's 'I will survive', I asked more questions. 'Do you ever get scared living with someone who's HIV positive?'

'Of course not!' John looked annoyed. 'I'm HIV negative and get tested regularly to check my status. HIV can only be transmitted by blood or sperm. You only get it if you have unsafe sex or share needles. Andy and I don't do those things.'

'How did he get it? If you don't mind me asking.'

'We're not sure.'

'That's so…' I didn't know how to end my sentence. 'Unfair.'

'Yes, but it's manageable. Andy and I have a good life together. He's made the right changes to manage his status. What's happened to so many gay men since the AIDS epidemic swept through our community has been horrendous or, as you say, unfair. It is. Andy and I have lost many dear friends.'

'I'm sorry, John,' I didn't know what else to say as I considered myself fortunate growing up in a time when there was a massive awareness campaign warning society about the virus. For the first time, it occurred to me that if I'd been born a few years earlier, I could have been one of the friends Andy and John had lost to AIDS. Neither of us said anything for a few seconds as 'I will survive' continued to play hauntingly. It was a song of strength and survival, just as the gay community was strong and a group of survivors, not just from AIDS but also from violence and abuse. I changed the subject. 'So…what's an open relationship?'

'It's an arrangement Andy and I have always had since we met in 1985. While we're together, it doesn't mean that we can't have sex with someone else outside of our relationship. Life's short. I'm not into letting opportunities pass me by. I don't think monogamy is all it's cracked up to be. That's why Andy doesn't mind me seeing so much of you, Nathan.'

John's words made me realise I had a lot to learn about my viewpoint of what a relationship could be, particularly if you were gay. In some ways, not being accepted by the mainstream society meant gay guys could write their own rules about what it meant to be loved and in relationships. I was glad that I had come out to John. There was something very authentic, honest, and unpretentious about him.

Before the end of our first semester, John invited me to participate in his open relationship. 'Next weekend, Andy is going to visit his family in Sydney. Want to stay the night at my place while he's away, just you and me?'

'Yeah!' I grinned as any horny queer eighteen-year-old teenager would to a chance to sleep with a handsome man as John.

John and Andy's home was a large, cement loft-style abode near Bangalow. It was a large concrete shell they were temporarily living in while construction had started on a new house on a plot of land that overlooked the river.

As night fell, John and I consumed a jar full of Tim Tams because we both had the munchies. This was after sharing a joint of locally grown weed. We were both naked. I got hard the minute he took my hand to lead me to the bed. It was like John had a magic touch. We kissed and pressed our bodies together. I loved every second of being with a real man. At the age of eighteen, I was still a virgin when it came to penetration. I'd never taken or given it. My fear of AIDS and shame about being gay had made me scared to try anything like that.

That's why my first night with John ended in nothing more explicit than a passionate embrace and masturbation, a very intense hand job. Laughing wasn't the only thing John did intensely.

After that night, I was hooked on John.

Luckily, John wanted to see me after lectures every day. He even stayed overnight once a week in my dorm room, sneaking out before my roommates got up in the morning. John joked that the experience made him feel like he was a naughty teenager again. The extreme age difference became more obvious not through sex but through subjects such as music. John tried to show me how trendy he was by asking if I liked the same music.

'Do you like Kraftwerk?'

'I like to draw,' I replied, clueless what John meant.

'No, I mean the German musical act, the pioneers of electronic dance music.'

'Never heard of them. I'm into Kylie Minogue.'

'In my day, the gay scene was all about Grace Jones. That's what we used to dance to in the bars on Oxford Street.'

'I know Grace Jones!' I replied to demonstrate how cultured I was. 'I saw her at a New Year's Eve RAT party in 1989 at 4am when I was sixteen years old at The Royal Hall of Industries!'

'You have no idea how ancient you just made me feel.' John grinned as he ran his hands through my hair playfully. John revealed that Andy had become concerned over John's infatuation with a much younger man. Their open relationship was becoming an openly hostile relationship. I saw the evidence of this when John took Brad, Claire, and I to the Tropical Fruits dance party promoted on Out FM.

The party was held at a church hall in the hinterland. A few hundred colourful people turned up. It was the entire local Northern Rivers gay and lesbian community ready to party till dawn under the glittering stars. The stars in the countryside shined ten times brighter than they did over the city lights of Sydney. I wondered if this was merely a natural phenomenon or was the visual intensity of the stars enhanced artificially by the acid trips Brad had scored for us, following a visit to Nimbin.

I couldn't wait to take that trip. It had been so long since I'd been high. I didn't hesitate. But it was Claire's first time, so she was understandably hesitant.

'Are you sure about this?' Claire asked.

'You'll be fine,' Brad assured Claire. 'You're with friends! We'll look out for you!'

'We'll be here if anything happens.' John smiled.

'Okay...' Claire put the paper trip on her tongue.

'I'll be here for you,' I promised Claire. 'If you feel frightened or strange in any way, let me know.'

The night was filled with wonder until John's partner, Andy, arrived. Andy was surrounded with John and Andy's mutual friends. Their mutual friends completely ignored John.

'Cradle snatcher!' Andy sneered before hugging an older man who also looked at John disapprovingly. Andy looked older than John and had grey hair. He didn't have a fit body like John did. He looked ill. I immediately realised that regardless of their open relationship, Andy wasn't the only one unimpressed with the reality of seeing John with a much younger man. I felt uneasy and the LSD did not help the situation one bit. I was feeling like I was responsible for breaking them up. I felt very bad.

'We shouldn't be together!' I broke free from John's embrace. 'You're in a relationship!'

'Don't worry,' John reassured me. 'Andy's just jealous I found you first.'

'I feel like I'm dividing the Northern Tablelands gay community.'

'It does seem that way!' Brad scolded me with a smirk. 'You big home-wrecker!'

I giggled, high on LSD. I'd never been called a homewrecker before. It sounded so old and from the 1950s. Bad made me laugh so easily.

'Totally! That was intense!' Claire giggled as the effects took hold.

'Andy will get over it,' John said, seemingly for his own benefit.

The morning after dancing all night in a country church hall, seeing heavenly visions of alternative middle-aged couples dancing together without a care in the world, we retired to The Homestead to come down. In the living room, Brad and Claire smoked cones and watched Rage, an endless loop of music videos on the ABC with a bunch of new friends from the party, people Michael had adopted during the night.

While everyone was distracted, John took the opportunity to sneak me into a spare bedroom that overlooked the hills as the sun rose. 'I want to fuck you!' He sounded serious.

This statement made me laugh. I was still high. 'Um… I'm not sure about that!' I was still fuzzy and felt a combination of emotions from apprehension to excitement. Even though I was horny and coming down off acid, I was nervous about the prospect. I wasn't sure I could do it. It seemed so unnatural. Or so I'd been made to believe all my life from school yard bullying.

John made a point of putting on a condom, but as he tried to enter me, it felt too intense.

'STOP! STOP! STOP!' I yelled

'But it wasn't even in!' John laughed, intensely as usual. 'In that case, why don't you fuck me?'

'Me?'

I wasn't sure I was ready for what John was proposing. Yet, as he leaned forward and braced his strong arms against the windowsill, I squeezed a condom over my dick for the very first time. John had a bubble-butt; it was round and tight. I felt weird doing it, but I figured it was about time. High on LSD, eighteen-year-old hormones surging and sleep deprived, the experience felt like a surreal dream, an outer body experience that became an inner body experience as I entered another masculine body. The intensity of being inside John made me breath heavily.

'Man! This is awesome!' My excitement built as my hands held on tight to John.

John moaned as I thrust forward. The sensation of being so close to another person for the first time was mind-blowing. I was breaking my gay virginity! I felt like I could go all morning, until John insisted and pleaded for me to let go.

'So, that's what all the fuss is about!' I said, sweating heavily, feeling elated and euphoric. No longer was I, as Madonna had sung, 'Like a virgin'.

COMING OUT

DURING THE FIRST semester break in the winter of 1991, I arranged to catch up with Tiffany in Sydney. Little did she know, I'd decided to tell her the truth. I'd been inspired by John to be honest about who I really was. Although, telling Tiffany was making me anxious. I had this notion she may react badly as we'd been a couple when we were younger.

Would she be mad at me for lying to her for so many years? There had been countless occasions when I should have told Tiffany I was gay. For example, when she first took me to a gay bar, The Exchange Hotel, when we were fifteen years old. That was the time I'd realised for sure I belonged to the gay half of the crowd. But I just hadn't been ready then. I had been too young and afraid. I had still been called faggot by school yard bullies in those days.

Telling Tiffany tonight was a good way to practice saying it out loud before I told the people that mattered most: my mum and dad. Doing it person by person, I came to appreciate the alternative method of dropping a bombshell at family gatherings, such as Mother's Day or Father's Day. This is how Brad said he'd broken the news to his parents when the whole family had been present on Christmas day for lunch.

'Best present I ever gave!' Brad grinned and he made me laugh with his devilish smile. 'Seriously, the looks on their faces were priceless.'

'How did they take the news?' I asked.

'Not exactly well. Mum accused me of deliberately ruining Christmas.'

The thought of Brad's ambush approach made my mind implode. The prospect of coming out in a public manner was too much pressure. I was too self-conscious for that method. That's why I opted to do it one by one. I had used a friend's letter to reveal the truth to my closest high school friends at Town hall after the High School Certificate. Anna, Lee, Simon, and Sarah had all taken it well. They have given me hugs and revealed they'd had their suspicions.

Determined to reveal the truth to Tiffany, I caught a bus down Oxford Street to Darlinghurst. Tiffany was waiting inside the Burdekin Hotel in Surry Hills. She was dressed in black fishnet stockings, a lace top, and a tight mini skirt. Her lips were painted red and eyes stylishly outlined in black charcoal. If I had been straight, I would have been so into Tiffany. She was too hot for most straight men. That's one of the reasons she hung out and partied on the gay scene.

Tiffany's smile lit up the bar the moment she saw me enter. We embraced in a big, loving hug and quickly caught up on what each other had been up to since the New Year's Eve RAT Party.

'How's your music career going?' I asked.

'It's radical!' Tiffany beamed as she took a sip from a bottle of Sub-Zero, an alcohol-pop drink. 'We're going to film a music video next month!'

'Wicked!'

'I've got a present for you!' Tiffany handed me a cassette tape marked 'Elemental demo one'.

'Wow. I can't wait to listen to it!'

'You've got to ring me the minute you've listened to it! I want to know what you think,' Tiffany insisted. 'So, what's university like?'

'It's fun. Made lots of new friends.'

'Anyone special?'

'Actually, there is.'

'So, what's she like?'

I hesitated. Tiffany had said she. She believed I was straight.

'Not, what you'd expect.' I looked away.

'What do you mean?' Tiffany looked intrigued.

All the while we'd been talking, the only thing on my mind was finding the right moment to come out. I guessed that this was it.

'Tiffany, I've have got something to tell you.' I had to stop and to take a big sip of beer. I had to break through a protective barrier I'd spent a lifetime building pretending I was honestly straight. I felt so nervous and dishonest now. I'd been very good at lying.

'What is it?' Tiffany laughed. 'Is she ugly or something?'

'Not exactly,' I responded as I could feel my heart beating faster. My cheeks flushed. The fear of Tiffany rejecting me took hold for some reason. 'I don't know how you will react to this but I'm–'

Tiffany began to giggle because I couldn't complete a single sentence.

I giggled a bit too, determined to get the truth out.

'You're what?' Tiffany demanded. 'Engaged?'

'No. I'm gay.'

The moment these words were confessed, Tiffany's eyes lit up as the revelation washed over. She clapped her hands over her mouth. 'Oh my God! It all makes sense to me now.' Tiffany sounded relieved. 'I think I always knew, but only subconsciously. Do you know how fucked up I was? I used to wonder why we'd never done it. Of course, you're too handsome to be straight. You're gay!'

Then came all the standard questions.

'When did you know?'

'Do your parents know?'

'Do you have a boyfriend?'

With my sexual orientation officially set straight, so to speak, I felt lighter, relieved, and at ease. I had nothing left to hide. Thankfully, Tiffany thought my news was good news. To Tiffany, it meant she wasn't unattractive after all. And it was not as big a deal as I'd always thought it would be. 'I'm so relieved!' I sighed with a giant smile. 'Now it's time to party. I have someone I want you to meet.'

'You do have a boyfriend!' Tiffany looked over-excited for a second.

'No. I wish! He's just a friend.' I grinned as we finished our drinks before heading to meet Brad at the Albury Hotel.

'Nice!' Tiffany commented upon seeing the bar packed with wall-to-wall men. The Albury Hotel was a paradise of the sweetest disco beats and schooners of beer being served by handsome and shirtless bar tenders, each of whom resembled the physical perfection of Roman gladiators. "I've never been down this part of Oxford Street before!' Tiffany yelled in my ear.

I found Brad with a small group of friends, necessitating some introductions. There was Emma. Emma gave Tiffany and I a welcoming hug. Emma was so short, even in platform heels, she was barely 5-feet-tall. She could barely see above the shoulders of the men crowded around her. Not that the men noticed her. They were all giving Brad the eye. I was still in awe how good-looking Brad was myself, with his natural sandy blonde hair, blue eyes, stubble on his perfect square jawline, and winning smile. Brad reminded me of the super-hot new actor from the film 'Thelma & Louise', who he ironically shared the same first name, Brad Pitt. Even the untouchable barmen serving drinks behind the bar were not immune from Brad's looks. They occasionally threw smiles in Brad's direction in between serving drinks and, I would later find out, free drinks on the house.

The next person Brad introduced was his best friend from primary school, Stevie.

'So, Nathan, I hear you're fresh out of the closet!' This was the first thing Stevie said to me.

'Yes, I'm a newbie at this whole gay thing,' I replied sharply. This made Brad and Stevie laugh out loud.

'Well sweetheart, I've been doing it, and I do mean doing-it, for some time!' Stevie announced proudly. 'Let me know if I can give you any pointers.'

'Thanks, doll. I probably need your advice!' I turned to Brad. 'You're so lucky you had a best friend growing up who was also gay.'

'Not that we knew it in high school,' Stevie corrected me, waving his hand flamboyantly and dramatically.

'It was only after we left school that we came out and admitted it,' Brad explained. 'It was when we started venturing from the Northern Beaches to Darlinghurst every weekend that we came clean.'

I introduced Tiffany as my best friend since we had been kids. Brad and Stevie kissed Tiffany hello.

'You are so good looking!' Tiffany beamed.

'Right back at you, love!' Stevie grinned and took a sip of beer.

'How did she take it?' Brad asked knowing tonight was the night I had chosen to come out.

'Really well,' I replied, full of happiness. 'I mean, she's here with me now in the best gay bar in town, so that's got to be a good sign.'

Tiffany knew what we were talking about. 'When Nathan told me, it was like something clicked. I loved Nathan as his girlfriend when we were kids. I always knew there was something about Nathan that was different from the other boys. I think that's what I loved most about him, and now that I know the truth, I'll still love him maybe even more! He's my new best gay friend.'

'Are you saying you're Nathan's new fag hag?' Stevie joked.

'Shut-up, Stewie!' Brad slapped Stewie's playfully as I moved in to give Tiffany a hug and kiss on the cheek.

Stevie remarked with sincerity, 'That's beautiful, Tiffany. You're so lovely. You guys are so cute.'

'Absolutely!' Brad agreed.

'So are you!' Tiffany didn't hold back. 'You guys should date; you'd make the cutest couple.'

'No, we're just friends.' Brad smiled shaking his head. 'I see Nathan like he's a younger brother. When I met him, I just knew! I was also there and in the closet about three years ago.'

'When did you come out?' Tiffany asked Brad.

'When he bumped into me in a steam room!' Stevie chimed in with a sneaky grin.

'A what?' Tiffany smiled curiously.

'A men-only space,' Brad explained. 'There was no way either of us could come up with a cover story standing there wearing only a towel.'

'It was pretty embarrassing!' Stevie sneered. 'I mean can you imagine this ugly man practically naked?'

Brad just waved his hand dismissively at Stevie's quip, while I got the impression that Stevie was deeply in love with his overly handsome former and unattainable high school best friend.

'Yes, I'm picturing it!' Emma giggled. 'What a couple of hunks!'

'Shut-up!' Brad seemed self-conscious for a second.

'Do you guys have boyfriends?' Tiffany asked.

'Not at the moment.' Brad grinned.

'But after tonight, who can say?' Stevie winked.

Brad and Stevie clinked their beer glasses together at the promise of what the night might hold, laughing to themselves. As the night progressed, I came to realise that flamboyant was an understatement when it came to describing Stevie. He was dressed in bright colours, wore foundation cream on his face, and had his hair gelled tightly back over his skull. He was a drag queen without a dress. Suddenly, a real life drag queen, Robyn Lee, began to perform in the middle of the bar. Her beautiful red hair and silver sequin gown flowed as she lip-synced to 'Gypsy Woman (La De Dee)' by Crystal Waters, with two muscular leather-clad back-up dancers.

'I've got to take a closer look!' Tiffany announced before pushing her way through a wall of men to reach the edge of the bar for a better view.

'Your friend sure is confident,' Emma commented. 'I'm going to follow her!'

'She sure is!' I agreed as Emma made her way to Tiffany, who was cheering at Robyn Lee with excitement.

'So, when are you going to tell your parents?' Brad asked me.

I shrugged. I didn't have an answer for this. I hoped to do it during the semester break. Yet I felt mildly anxious just at the thought of it. All I could think was, what if they cut me off? No more university. I'd be on the streets.

'You look nervous!' Brad grinned.

'I just don't know how they'll take it. They're very old-fashioned,' I told my new best gay friend.

'Mothers know,' Brad assured me. 'Trust me. All mothers know.'

DON'T CRY MAMA (DCM)

BY THE END of the drag show, it was past midnight. Even though it was winter and freezing outside, many patrons of the Albury Hotel had taken to drinking and smoking cigarettes on the pavement in the cold night air. I followed Brad, Emma, Stevie, and Tiffany as we pushed our way through the mob to continue our journey into the night.

We made our way towards Taylor Square. Cars jammed the asphalt of Oxford Street. The reflection of red break and blinding headlights illuminated the pathway forward. All the bright young things were pounding the pavement, ready for Saturday night fun. The next stop was DCM. Along the way, Stevie and Emma ran a verbal commentary on the sights passing by, throwing insults left, right, and centre, which Tiffany and I found so humorous. My stomach began to ache from laughter by the time we reached our dance-all-night destination.

Stevie's alcohol-fuelled dialogue involved shouting at complete strangers who were cute. 'Hey handsome, I'll be at DCM. You can catch me there later, if you're lucky.'

'Yeah, in the toilets, you dirty slut!' Emma shouted back, then gave Stevie a nudge in his ribs with a knowing laugh.

'Where else?' Stevie owned his dirty slut status.

But what impressed me most was when they yelled back at the aggressive heterosexual men who yelled faggot from their revved-up cars filled with the type of men who deliberately drove to the golden gay mile simply to hurl abuse at anyone they saw.

'Poofter!' they took turns yelling hatefully.

'Thanks for the compliment!' Stevie yelled back.

'Go back to the boring suburb you crawled in from, jerkoffs!' Emma told them where to go.

Clearly, these men weren't used to being abused back by a tiny girl. They had no come-back.

'Done him, him, and him too!' Stevie pointed at each of the young men glaring from their car windows.

'Why do they drive to this street if they're offended by what they see?' Tiffany asked in all seriousness.

'Because they're not really offended. They're all closet homosexuals, I'm sure of it.' Brad grinned.

Tiffany and I shared a look of revelation, nodding at Brad's wisdom about those awful men. As we strolled down the pavement, it felt like we were all on the brink of something fabulous and dangerous.

'Is it always like this?' I asked Brad. Brad nodded with a smirk before we joined the queue outside the entrance to DCM. It was well past midnight when the bouncer nodded for our clan to climb the stairs to the club.

The black décor inside made the atmosphere feel heavy and dense. It was busy inside, and the music was loud. DCM was Sydney's answer to New York's 1970s Studio 54, but with far fewer celebrities sprinkled through the crowd. But I soon came to realise that the steamy club was packed with plenty of scene queens who believed they were celebrities.

This included Stevie and Emma, who both behaved like they were the main attraction. 'No pictures or autographs!' Stevie announced as we entered the crowded bar. The in-crowd just stared back at Stevie like he was mad. While others wondered if they should know who he was after such a dramatic entrance. An easy mistake to make given most of the patrons were on hallucinogens.

Before hitting the dance floor, it was down to business: time to purchase pills. Our clan scored from Stevie and Emma's trusty dealer. To my surprise, the dealer turned out to be a boy who used to be in the old In Full Effect crew from Kadoma Café in Kings Cross. He was part of the group of drug dealers that Tiffany and I had bought pills from in 1989. Now in 1991, our dealer, Mark, was far more undercover as a drug dealer, collecting cash and handing over pills under the cover of a black table in the corner cubicle, eyes on the bar to ensure nothing suspicious was happening.

The location where Mark set-up shop for his illegal operation was genius. From the booth in the corner of the bar, he had a view towards the dance floor. It was packed with patrons happily dancing and waving their arms in the air after having sampled Mark's merchandise.

I could tell Tiffany was instantly attracted to Mark's boy-next-door good looks. She was smiling at him and swaying slowly side to side. I also thought Mark was cute. He had straight brown hair and wore a tight, white Bond's singlet that revealed bulging biceps. One of his big biceps rested around a skinny, drug-fucked chickee-babe who, in my opinion, was wearing too much make-up.

It appeared Mark was one of the few straight men in the establishment. He was a straight guy who'd cornered the market dealing designer drugs to the queer crowd. Stevie collected our cash and scored several ecstasy pills from Mark under the table as Tiffany struck up a conversation with the club's handsome dealer.

'Do you remember me?' Tiffany asked.

'You look like a girl I used to know.' Mark squinted and thought hard but couldn't remember Tiffany's name. 'Weren't you seeing Eddie back in the day?'

'Yes, that was me!' Tiffany grinned with excitement. 'What ever happened to Eddie? I don't see him out anymore.'

'Didn't you hear?' Mark said flatly. 'Eddie died of an overdose.'

'No!' Tiffany covered her mouth in shock.

'Smack.'

'Shit! That's so sad!' Tiffany sat down next to the girl by Matt's side and still looked shocked. Through Tiffany and Mark's conversation, I learnt that most of the old In Full Effect crew were in prison or unemployed now. It was too depressing, so I followed the rest of the clan as they headed for the bar to buy a bottle of water to swallow the little pink pills purchased from Mark. It was the first ecstasy pill I had taken in two years, since I had gone cold turkey to get through the HSC. While I hoped none of us would overdose, I grew excited knowing what to expect as I swallowed the bitter tasting pill.

An hour later, on the dance floor, I slipped into a familiar state of altered reality, a realm in which my friends turned into a bunch of celebrities dancing under the mirror balls. From our vantage point, we spent the evening admiring flawless muscle-boys dancing tirelessly around us.

Brad gave me a hug and yelled, 'I'm glad we became friends!'

'Me too!' I moved in to kiss Brad on the lips. But in that moment, Brad moved away to dance because he loved the song the DJ was playing, Nomad's '(I wanna give you) Devotion'. This left me standing still like a statue, ready to kiss a pair of lips that were no longer there. In this pose, my eyes were drawn to a blurry vision of one of the club's main attractions. It was the same guy I'd seen dancing on the podium the first time I had come to DCM with Anna, Lee, and Sarah, the one the boys had cheered at, *Dom*. There he was dancing in the same spot, displaying his well-built, six-foot-five physique that seemed to defy gravity as he moved energetically above the crowd.

There were two podiums on opposite ends of the packed dance floor at DCM, and it was clearly a big deal to be on one of them. Dom's footballer build ensured his towering figure could not be missed as he bopped up and down on the podium in quick secession. At first, I thought Dom was another appearance by the National Rugby League legend Ian Roberts, but then I realised that Dom just looked like Ian. On E, I thought Dom was amazing and desirable.

To my surprise, Dom noticed me staring at him adoringly, and my heart raced as we made eye contact. We checked each other out just for a brief second. It was a moment that seemed to last for a lifetime, until to the techno beat of the club mix of Madonna's 'Rescue me' distracted Dom from the sight of my longing stare. He returned to performing for his appreciative audience.

ON THE RECORD

27 NOVEMBER 1991

I CONTINUED TO LISTEN, feeling uneasy at what Dom had to say during the police interview.

'I want you to know you're not obliged to say anything unless you wish to do so, but whatever you say will be electronically recorded and may be used in evidence. Do you understand that?'

'Yes, I do.'

'Dom, I now show you a voucher for Aussie Boys Paddington, card number 5353 1234 4321 0987, dated 14 September at 14:55, totalling $139.80. Have you ever been to Aussie Boys Paddington?'

'Yes, quite frequently.'

'And what can you tell me about that signature?'

'I assume it was signed by Tiffany.'

'And can you recall what was purchased on that voucher?'

'No, I can't, as I can't recall if I was there or not.'

'Okay. I'm now going to ask you questions in relation to these 26 Mastercard vouchers. The first one is for a total value of $126. A signature appears at the bottom of the voucher. What can you tell me about that voucher?'

'That I didn't sign the voucher. That I didn't sign any of the vouchers as it is a female card!' Dom's voice burst with frustration from being asked what seemed *like the same question for the one-hundredth time. IIt sounded like Dom was trying his best to keep calm.*

I could imagine how self-conscious Dom felt, knowing he was being recorded.

When Dom spoke, he tried to sound like a professional banker, and not like a common criminal.

'Look, the signature was authorised by Tiffany. I'm not aware of the purchases made or if I was there with her at the time. I'm not aware if the goods were for herself or myself or for anyone else.'

'I see. Can you tell me who signed the signature at the bottom of the voucher?'

'Tiffany. She signed every voucher.'

'And how do you know that?'

'Well, every voucher I saw was signed by a female name.'

'Did you make any arrangement prior to entering each store as to which goods were going to be purchased?'

'Tiffany said to me I could go in with her and she'd buy things for me, or I could go in first, pick an item, and she'd go in after me and purchase it.'

'Did you know at the time when you came to this arrangement that it was wrong?'

'Yes, I did.'

'Did you know that the goods that were purchased using this illegitimate voucher were purchased illegally?'

'Yes, I did. And as I said in the interview given to the bank and to my manager, I was not stable at all at the time.'

'What goods did you receive in respect of these vouchers?'

'I don't remember. As I said, it was over 3 months ago. I wouldn't remember.'

'Did you keep any of the goods purchased?'

'No, not that I'm aware of.'

'Can you tell me why you can't remember? A few months ago isn't that long a time. Can you tell me why your memory is failing you in this regard?'

'As I said, I was very distraught. I was both physically and mentally ill at the time, and under a lot of stress, and financial stress.'

'Right. Um, do you remember how Tiffany purchased goods with the card? Did you see her sign vouchers for this card?'

'Yes, I did.'

'Do you remember roughly how many times you saw her sign vouchers?'

'No. I wouldn't.'

'You were present in the stores at the time. Was it correct that you were with her when she signed for this stolen card?'

'Correct.'

'Can you tell me, to your knowledge, was this card in any other person's possession?'

'No. Not that I'm aware of.'

'Can you tell me, on this date in question, was any other person with you and Tiffany when you made these purchases?'

'Yes, there was. There was Nathan, who knew nothing about the card being stolen. He just assumed it was Tiffany's. We pretended to him it was Tiffany's.'

'Can you tell me who Nathan is?'

'He's my boyfriend or my gay lover, whatever you want to address him as.'

'So, Nathan knew nothing about the falseness of the card?'

'No. He was under the impression it was Tiffany's.'

ONE BIG INCESTUOUS FAMILY

JULY 1991 - DCM

ALL NIGHT, I watched Dom dance on top of the podium. He busted moves such as 'the running man' and then posed like Madonna in the Vogue video clip when the electronic beats paused in the euphoric Tony King angelic remix of Kylie Minogue's 'Keep on pumpin' it'. In my euphorically altered state, I wondered what this dancing Adonis would do next.

In contrast, Brad's friend Stevie watched with a look of ridicule. 'Who does she think she is?' Stevie groaned in reference to Dom's dancing.

'One of Madonna's back-up dancers!' Emma teased.

'Totally!' Brad agreed in frustration. 'I shouldn't have to put up with seeing that. Not while I'm on a break.'

'Oh, for sure!' Emma agreed. 'Vogue in so nineteen-ninety!'

'Love, it's now nineteen-ninety-one!' Stevie yelled towards Dom's direction. But against the booming techno beat of Erasure's 'Love to hate you', Dom couldn't hear a word of the ridicule being hurled at him. Dom was on a mission to entertain his adoring audience.

'I think he's a good dancer!' I blurted out feeling extra loving on the love drug I hadn't been on in years. MDMA was making me believe everything was amazing, including Dom.

'Oh, please!' Brad's jaw dropped. 'He's completely annoying!'

'Such an attention seeker!' Emma agreed. 'Honestly, that queen is up there every night doing the same crappy moves.'

'I think he's got a lease on that podium,' Stevie mocked Dom.

'I heard he's homeless,' Emma giggled. 'If he stops dancing, they'll evict him.'

Our group shared a laugh as we returned to dancing with the other clubbers grooving on the crammed dance floor. When I looked away from Dom's silhouette, I noticed that Tiffany was uncharacteristically absent from the dance floor. I looked around and saw Tiffany was still seated in the booth with Mark. The next time my gaze moved away from Dancing Dom, I saw Tiffany was making out with Mark; they were kissing like their lives depended on it.

'She's a fast mover!' Stevie commented following my gaze. I nodded in agreement, and felt a twinge of jealously. Everyone was getting kisses but me.

Later in the evening, Brad introduced another old school friend of his who had just gotten off work. 'Nathan, this is my ex-boyfriend, Dan.' Brad grinned with his arm around a handsome, tall, and fit guy who looked about twenty years old. Dan had short brown hair, brown eyes, and very pale skin. He was wearing a black singlet and had a lean muscular frame.

I smiled and Dan took the opportunity to strike up a conversation, asking what seemed like unusual, offbeat questions at 3am such as:

'How do you know this lot?'

'What's your story?'

'How did you get roped into being here tonight?'

On drugs, my brain was wired to respond with a quick smart-ass reply to each question:

'Just lucky I guess.'

'I just came out, of the closet that is!'

'I'm easily led.'

'I see!' Dan grinned. 'You'll fit in just fine with us.'

High on ecstasy, I enjoyed chatting to just about anyone. But when that *anyone* happened to be a tall, dark, handsome stranger, the enjoyment became somewhat of a thrill.

I liked how Dan had a similar sense of humour as Stevie and Emma, only a bit darker when he commented, 'You know that we're all just one big incestuous family. We all sleep with each other on a nightly basis, kind of like the Manson family minus the murders.' Dan's eye twinkled with a devilish smile.

'As long as you keep it in the family and don't murder anyone.' I smiled in response to Dan's dark side, letting Dan know I was ready to play his game. Dan revealed he was an aspiring journalist. I let him know I was also studying journalism.

'Wow! We have so much in common,' I gushed as Dan said, in between getting articles published, he moonlighted in the hospitality industry as a supervising waiter at the Gazebo Hotel Banquet Hall. He had just gotten off work at 2am.

'I recently split from my boyfriend,' Dan yelled in my ear. 'I'm ready to find the next one.'

'Look no further!' I blurted out completely unfiltered on ecstasy.

'You're not ready for me!' Dan looked deep into my eyes and then he leaned in for a kiss, but stopped. 'You're as cute as Brad said you were. That almost never happens.'

'What? Really?' I was taken back. 'What normally happens? What else did Brad say?'

'Just that you're a newbie, inexperienced, and I'm to be on my best behaviour with you, apparently.'

'So, this is you on your best behaviour?'

'Afraid so.' Dan smiled as his eyes scanned the flashing lights above before returning to look me in the eye. 'Want to get out of here?' None of Brad's friends could believe how fast Dan had scored with me. Or had I scored with Dan? The truth was that no one in Brad's incestuous family slept with one another all the time, not on a regular basis, the way Dan had implied. He had been kidding. What Dan had said was an urban club myth. Until I came along. Contrary to the fantasy account Dan had painted for me about Brad's friends' debauched lifestyle, the truth was most of them went home alone.

I was flattered when Dan invited me to go home with him. Dan seemed so down-to-earth compared to Brad's other friends. Being high on ecstasy for the first time in years, I fell in love with Dan overnight, even though Dan wasn't like all the typical body boys that danced the night away at DCM.

Dan didn't have a fake tan. His skin was so white and pale. His body was natural. He didn't have steroid-bloated muscles. His body was tight and fit from working shifts at the Gazebo and being on his feet all night.

The walls of Dan's apartment were covered in Kylie Minogue posters, some that had the actual lady's signature on them. I was so impressed. To come down following working to 2am and after picking up me up at DCM at 3am, Dan shared a bong with me. The bong was part of Dan's routine to relax after work and meeting strangers at DCM.

The dope wasn't nearly as strong as what I was used to from Nimbin.

Once we were both sufficiently stoned, Dan led me to his bedroom.

We got naked and pressed our bodies and erections together on his waterbed. Sure enough, and true to his opening pick-up line, I joined the 'incestuous family'. Being a newbie and high on illicit substances, I drove myself wild with the experience of having so much to play with during the final hours of an enlightening night. Dan had the longest dick I'd ever seen.

KEN'S

BEFORE THE MID-YEAR university semester break was over, I caught up with two other university friends. The first was John, who was also visiting his Sydney buddies to let off some steam. Fortunately for me, John made sure he found time to catch up with his younger man. I was excited at the prospect of meeting up with John in Sydney, even though I felt like I was two-timing, having started something new with Dan.

After Dan and I had spent our first night together, we met for coffee. For a laugh, Dan and his university buddies took me to Taronga Zoo on acid. We each took LSD and went day tripping. We were all in hysterics watching the animals in an altered state, hallucinating and trying to keep it together so we didn't get removed by Security.

I also slept with Dan two more times before John arrived. That's why I felt like I was cheating on Dan. Especially as I was hoping that my encounters with Dan might become something more serious.

Deep down, I suspected my relationship with John didn't have much of a future, given John already had a long-term partner. Yet, there was something about John that I was drawn to. It was a feeling I had when I was with him, that I had a lot to learn from my relationship with the handsome, mature student. When we caught up, it turned out I did have plenty to discover.

'Have you ever been to Ken's?' John asked me as we drove away from Oxford Street in his blue ute.

'Ken's?' I had no idea what John was referring to. I wondered if it were a nightclub I'd never been to before.

'Then let me take you.' John grinned from behind the wheel. He pulled up on an ordinary busy suburban road in Kensington. It was a suburb behind Centennial Park, not far from where I had grown up. 'See that?' John pointed to a brown brick building across the road that had rainbow flags on the awning. 'It's Sydney's best kept secret.'

'What do you mean?' I asked, slightly confused upon seeing the sign above the door, which read, Ken's Karate Klub.

'It's a gay sauna.' John grinned enthusiastically. 'Practically every man in Sydney's been there at some point. Want to see what it's like?'

'A gay sauna?'

'Yes, a men-only space. It's like a gay nightclub, only it goes twenty-four hours, and you only wear a towel. Or nothing at all, it's entirely up to you!' John laughed intensely at his own joke. I didn't laugh along. I was apprehensive at the idea. 'Come on.' John cut the ignition and got out of the car. I followed him towards the brown brick building. The front door opened to reveal a narrow flight of ascending stairs. We walked up the staircase, which led to a booth protected by white metal bars with a half-naked man sitting behind a cash register. I wondered what the hell I was doing. 'Two please,' John handed over two twenty-dollar bills.

The half-naked and somewhat muscular man casually passed two white towels under the bars. The towels came with two numbered locker keys attached to red wristbands. The man pressed a button that buzzed open a second security door.

John took one of the towels, a locker key, and pushed the security door open.

I copied John, and grabbed the other towel and key. I followed him into the next room, which was filled with wall-to-wall lockers. It looked like a gym locker room. There were a few other men inside. Some appeared to be getting dressed, tying up their shoelaces, and others seemed to be getting undressed, unbuttoning their shirts. They just looked like ordinary guys, not particularly gay. Just like any average man you'd see on the street.

John headed for his locker. I followed closely, unsure of what to expect, but curious to find out. As John began to take off his shoes, I did the same and felt self-conscious getting naked in front of complete strangers. Even in high school, getting changed for gym class in the boys' locker room had filled me with anxiety. I didn't like strangers to get the opportunity to check out the size of my dick and balls. Although, by comparison to some on display in the locker-room, I had nothing to be ashamed of.

I wasted no time in wrapping the towel around my waist.

'Ready?' John grinned at how visibly nervous I had become within a short space of time. 'You okay?'

'Yeah,' I lied. I was fully freaking out. I wanted to have sex with John so bad but didn't expect it to be in a place like this. Exiting the change room, I followed John as he entered a corridor that was dimly lit with a red light. Other men, also only wearing white towels, were wandering by slowly. Their body language was longing and seductive.

John and I headed down a flight of stairs that were opposite a glowing blue indoor swimming pool with two men in it. Both men were kissing in a naked embrace. Downstairs, I followed John through a labyrinth filled with corridors and wandering men wearing white towels around their waist. It was like a maze surrounded by small cubicles, each with only a black foam mat, a dispenser filled with lubricant, and condoms.

I did my best to stay close to John as we strolled past an assortment of men waiting by the open doors. Some were completely naked and playing with themselves while waiting for anyone to join in the fun. Soon, I felt someone's fingers take hold of my hand. To my surprise, it was a reasonably attractive, hairy-chested young man about my own age. He nodded his head towards an empty cubicle for me to join him. Part of me wanted to go in with him, but I pulled my hand back.

The beat of Alison Limerick's 'Where love lives' played from speakers overhead, but not loud enough to cover the sounds of men having sex in the booths. I could hear grunts and moans. The unmistakable aroma of amyl-nitrate hung in the air.

'He wants you to join him!' John whispered in my ear.

'I don't want to!' I whispered back feeling incredibly self-conscious.

No one else was saying anything; it was all about eye contact and one's physical appearance. John smiled and we continued to explore the rest of what Ken's had to offer. We entered a room where a large screen projected an X-rated hardcore gay porn video to an audience of men laying around on black vinyl mats. Some were openly masturbating to the vision of a hard-core gay porn. On screen, a man with a huge dick was engaged in lewd acts with a muscular man in the Australian bushland.

On the other end of the labyrinth was a set of showers, where a man with an amazing physique and well-hung cock soaped up his body under the jet stream. Beyond the muscle man was a fogged-up glass door which opened to a large steam room. Inside the steam room it was hard to see from the heavy mist.

I waited for my eyes to adjust to the dimly lit, hot, and wet space. More half-naked men were seated enjoying the steam while others had sex in plain sight of anyone who cared to watch or join in. It was like a slice of an ancient Roman orgy in the heart of modern Sydney. John followed me. No one spoke.

I felt someone rub my buttocks as another man reached for my cock. With all this available talent on offer, I was overwhelmed and couldn't believe such a place existed. At eighteen years old, I wasn't ready for what Ken's had to offer. With my mind blown and my heart pounding, I took John's hand and led him back outside the steam room.

'Can we have sex? Just you and me.'

'Sure!' John smiled and pressed his lips against mine. John led me towards an empty cubical where we continued to kiss passionately as our towels dropped to the floor.

ALL MOTHERS KNOW

THE OTHER UNIVERSITY friend I spent time with during the break was my short-lived girlfriend, Claire. I invited Claire to stay at my parents' home so I could take her out clubbing and show her what the Sydney scene was like. A few days after Claire arrived, I had a chat with my mum over breakfast while Claire showered in the upstairs guest bathroom.

My mum took this moment as an opportunity to reveal she'd sensed something wasn't quite right about Claire. Even as Claire recovered from her mental health episode, she did have moments where she acted differently. Somehow, my mum had noticed something about Claire, and she confided, 'Claire's a little unusual.'

In that instant, I thought this was my big chance to talk about things closer to home; that was unusual. Brad's words echoed through my mind, *'All mothers know…'*

I desperately wanted to get my mother to admit she knew I was gay. I started by telling mum how nice it was of her to let Claire stay. "Yes, I know what you're saying about Claire. She has a condition."

'I could tell something was different about Claire,' Mum admitted in a hushed voice, adding, 'Poor girl and her poor parents.'

'Can you also sense that there is something *different* about me?'

'*Different* about you?'

'Like…me being gay.'

Mum looked lost.

'No…' Mum momentarily frozen as the news set in adding, 'I had no idea.'

'Come on, you had no idea?' I grinned even though my heart started to race. I did my best to keep my voice jovial, acting like announcing I was gay wasn't as big a shock as mum was making it out to be.

'You could give us AIDS!' My mum looked horrified.

I rolled my eyes in protest, annoyance, and disbelief. 'I'm not going to share needles or sleep with you, Mum, so I don't see how that's possible.' I'd had an inclination my mum would have a hard time accepting I was gay. But this was beyond my worst nightmares. She really did have a talent for going straight to the most drastic eventuality. Mum's upbringing hadn't been in the city. She was from a religious background, growing up on a remote Queensland farm with her three siblings. I had known there would be a possibility she wouldn't take my secret very well. Where was the chorus of, *'You're my son, and no matter what you do, I will always love you.'*?

'We'll never have grandchildren!' This was the next ridiculous thing mum had to say.

'You don't know that!' I was deeply annoyed at the pure ignorance slipping out of my mother's mouth as the gravity of what I'd told her hit home hard. 'You never know. I could donate sperm to a girlfriend like Claire, or decide to have a child with a couple of lesbians.'

'That's no way to have a child!' Mum cut me off. 'You're never to tell your father!'

'Fine!' On that point, we agreed for the time being. After my mother's reaction, I wasn't keen to find out what my more openly homophobic father's reaction would be. When I was fourteen years old dad had told me, *'Gays are what is wrong with the world!'* This was in response to seeing footage of the Sydney Gay and Lesbian Mardi Gras broadcast on the evening news. At the time, I'd nodded in agreement, knowing that I was queer. Dad had unknowingly told me I was what was wrong with the world.

Coming out to Mum had not gone according to plan. Unfortunately, not all mothers know. Or want to know.

I was surprised at my mum's reaction of utter denial about me being gay, given she once found some pornographic magazines in my bedroom closet when I was sixteen years old. In the year after I had my first sexual experience with a twenty-one-year-old man named Campbell, I'd stopped going to Oxford Street to pick up men. Instead, I'd snuck off to Kings Cross to buy copies of 'Inches' magazine with my pocket money. 'Inches' had featured a hunky male model, shirtless and looking very provocative. There was no mistaking what my sexual orientation was, given I'd had a collection of these XXX magazines in my closet. It was hardcore evidence I was gay.

Like any healthy, red-blooded teenage boy whose hormones were off the charts, I used to get fixated on the sordid pages of my secret magazine collection rather than do homework, and the dopamine hit that came from looking at them. That was until my mum unexpectedly discovered my stash of macho magazines when she went through my closet for some reason. I almost died when she told me, 'I found those magazines with a *very* dirty man on the cover.'

I had said nothing, petrified and beyond embarrassed, knowing my secret was out. I'd felt the ground sink. Mum knew! When my mum found *those* magazines, I'd felt intense shame about being gay. Mum had reinforced the shame I felt being bullied at school for being a fag. She'd known for sure I was gay because I liked those magazines.

'I never want to see them again!' Mum had informed me sternly at the time. 'Do you understand?'

While I had been horrified and humiliated that my mother had discovered my gay porn mag collection, I had also been somewhat confused by her response. All she'd said of the matter was, *'I never want to see them again.'* And that was it. She hadn't used it as an opportunity to ask if I was gay. There's been no discussion about the birds and the bees, or the bees and the bees. She never spoke of it again, and neither did I. We had both lived in denial.

At the time, I had several things going on in my teenage life. My group of friends were venturing to Club Hordern for dance parties each weekend. I was covering up a developing an amphetamine habit while trying to keep up with schoolwork at the same time. Those magazines had been my release from the pressure. And my amphetamine habit, I now suspected, had been nothing more than an escape from the reality of my situation, living in the closet.

Now that I had finally admitted the truth to my mother and come out, her reaction was, yet again, to pretend it had never happened by insisting I never reveal the truth to my father. To stay in the closet where I'd once hidden those dirty magazines. To pretend to be heterosexual as far as Dad was concerned.

'I mean it, Nathan. You're *not* to tell your father. It will kill him. You know how he feels about homosexuals!'

I was glad Claire was staying with us, mainly because her presence provided a welcome distraction for my mum about what we'd just discussed.

'Morning!' Claire joined us in the kitchen, all smiles.

'What would you like for breakfast, dear?' Mum smiled back at Claire like a Stepford wife, friendly and robotic.

'Just a grapefruit, please.' Claire smiled politely and then sensed there was serious tension in the room. Claire gave me a sideways glance, as if to say *what's up?*

I just angrily rolled my eyes.

After breakfast, I confided in Clare about what had just taken place. Her response instantly made me feel better.

'Is that what she said?' Claire burst into laughter and had to cover her mouth with both hands to calm down. 'Oh my god! Nathan, you've got to admit that's funny. You could give your mum AIDS. Really? Come on!'

'Kind of an over-reaction, hey?'

'I can't wait to hear what your father has to say next! Will your dad think you could get him pregnant?'

'I'm not to tell him.'

'Why?' Claire seemed puzzled. 'That's ridiculous! You have absolutely nothing to be ashamed of. It's their problem if they have a problem with it.'

'Yeah, sure, but what if they stopped paying for my degree?'

'That won't happen, Nathan.'

'Also, I'm not to have babies with you, Claire.'

Claire covered her mouth again to muffle her laughter.

'But, Nathan, you and I would make the most beautiful babies! If I haven't had any by thirty, I want you to donate your sperm. I'm serious!"

JOIN US THIS AFTERNOON

BEFORE RETURNING TO Lismore, Claire and I took a walk on the wild side. She was eager to visit Oxford Street at night and explore the gay scene in Sydney. To celebrate our last Saturday night before returning to university, we dressed in 70s-inspired disco kitsch stripes we'd discovered at the Saint Vinnie's store in Paddington.

We met Brad at the Albury Hotel with his friends, and the rest of the night became a blur. We took acid in the ladies' toilets at The Albury Hotel. We buzzed from the dance floor of DCM to the much smaller venue of The Taxi Club.

Brad said The Taxi Club was also known as *The Star Wars Bar* because it was like the scene from Star Wars with so many unusual characters drinking in a galaxy, far, far away. It was tiny, pokey, and above all, loads of fun with the steepest steps of any nightclub known to humanity. After The Taxi Club, we crossed the street, and discovered it was daylight outside. We entered the Flinders Hotel where the beat was still pumping. You could hear it from the outside on the pavement.

'Yay!' Brad announced as he pushed both pub doors wide open. 'It's a recovery party!' Inside they were playing Kylie Minogue's, 'What do I have to do?' There weren't many people left standing except for us and some men dancing on the bar. While the crowd had thinned, the venue had an atmosphere of still being in full swing. Claire was fascinated by two young, fit, blond men. They were both only wearing jeans and were dancing shirtless on top of the bar. They looked like clones.

The bartenders didn't seem to mind the boys dancing on the bar. I think it was because both men were proudly showing off stunningly smooth upper bodies ripped with muscle and dripping with sweat.

'Why don't you get up there?' Claire asked.

'I'm not as hot as them!' I confessed.

'Also, too much effort!' Brad waved his hand dismissively before we settled for dancing on the sticky floor below.

At eighteen years old, while my body was lean, I had not been through the rigor of a regular gym cycle of pumping iron with steroids to look like the boys dancing on the bar. I had a six-pack of abdominal muscles with skinny arms and a flat chest. Nor did I frequent tanning beds to achieve that sun-kissed appearance, even in the middle of winter. I was also yet to regularly visit a beautician to have my fine chest and stomach hair ripped from my body with hot wax. I looked far too natural and ordinary to jump up and dance freely on top of the bar without attracting what I imagined would be ridicule from the few remaining queens left inside the establishment.

Or so I thought, until I attracted the attention of the blond muscle boys. All I did was dance with drug induced gay abandon in the corner of the bar. I think it was my gyrating hips to the beat of the second Kylie Minogue song for the morning shift, 'I guess I like it like that', that captured the muscle boys' attention. One of the handsome blond boys hopped off the bar, wrote something down on a bar coaster, and handed it to me with a big grin.

Even with blurred vision, I could tell in the darkness that on the bar coaster was a phone number and a message, 'Join us this afternoon'. Upon reading this, my heart raced at the prospect of acrobatic sexual activities with the attractive young men, and the thought of being in bed with both at the same time. But by the time I had processed the message, the blond boy had returned to his elevated position dancing on the bar with his equally blond partner.

'I can't!' I yelled at him. But he couldn't hear me over the blasting music and their obviously drugged state. They just looked at me and smiled like they knew I was a *sure thing*. The reason I couldn't join them was because I had to be on the 4pm XPT cross-country train bound for Lismore with Brad and Claire. We had classes to attend tomorrow. Train tickets weren't transferrable.

'I can't join you!' I tried again, desperate to get their attention. The blonds just smiled in pure ecstasy as they danced like they were superstars. 'I'm leaving this afternoon!' I tried to explain in vain. All I got in return from the boy who'd handed me the message was a *call me* motion as he placed his hand against the side of his head in the shape of a phone.

Coming down from four weeks of drug taking, coming out, and meeting colourful new acquaintances, I wondered why I was such a goody two-shoes when it came to this once-in-a-lifetime invitation.

That afternoon, instead of partying with the two muscular blonds, I was on the verge of passing out in a train seat from a combination of exhaustion and a sleeping pill Brad had kindly given me. I vacantly watched the Australian countryside rush by outside the XPT train window while listening to Tiffany's demo tape on my Walkman. Tiffany's vocals were good, and the songs could easily be played in a club. However, it was difficult to focus on the music because I kept thinking that I should have stayed one more day.

I wondered what it would have been like to spend the afternoon with those two perfectly good-looking blond men. From the looks on their faces, it had been clear they were certain I would call and join them. They probably did that sort of thing all the time and never experienced someone not calling. They must have thought I was playing *hard to get*. Then again, I thought as I drifted into sleep, I could have dodged a *viral bullet*. Being as young as I was, incredibly horny, and seriously out of it, I suspected I could have easily been convinced to try some very unsafe sex by the two incredibly attractive and obviously experienced young men.

~

The heavy comedown hit the moment the sleeping pill wore off, and I found myself with Brad and Claire back in our university's country town of Lismore.

It was a sobering experience. At 2am, we dragged our luggage along the street towards Brad's shared home. It was walking distance from the train station. This way, we avoided a line of students waiting for the few taxis available in the sleepy country town.

I ended up crashing with Brad on a double mattress laid on the floorboards, while Claire took the sofa in the living room. Even though I was curious to find out what it would be like to have sex with Brad, nothing happened. We were both exhausted and I had come to accept I simply wasn't his type.

DESPERATE LEFTOVER

AFTER A MONTH of parting on the Oxford Street gay scene, Lismore and university didn't stack up by comparison. The campus seemed smaller than I remembered. I couldn't wait for the next semester break. I decided to use my time away from Sydney wisely and joined the local gym. This was so I could get my body up to scratch with what had now become the standard physique for gay boys: round shoulders, big biceps, a tight lean chest with defined pectoral muscles, and a six-pack of abdominal muscles.

John eagerly volunteered to become my personal trainer. Under his guidance and with a lot of effort, I started to notice in the gym mirror that my chest and biceps were becoming more defined. I was ready for Oxford Street.

'But don't forget that your legs, thigh, and calf muscles are also very sexy,' John advised. 'There's nothing less attractive than a guy with a big chest and chicken legs.'

'Chicken legs?'

'Big upper body but sticks for legs.'

Fortunately, I had developed solid calf muscles from speed walking up the track from campus to the dorms daily. My legs were the most muscular part of my body.

Seeing Brad again for the first time in a while in the university café, I noticed he seemed distracted and was dreaming of Sydney. Specifically, about a boy he'd met named Ricky.

'He's so cute!' Brad gushed, showing a photo taken of the two of them at The Californian Café. Brad wasn't exaggerating. Ricky looked like a Calvin Klein model named Marky Mark. Ricky was tanned, had a nice muscular torso, piercing light blue eyes, thick brown hair, full lips, and a square jaw line. It figured that Brad would end up with someone that was also impossibly good looking. Ricky had the body I was hoping to achieve with some extra effort at the gym.

'Hard to believe he's only seventeen.' Brad sighed.

'Bullshit. He looks much older!' I took a closer look at the photo, and realised that I wasn't too young for Brad after all, just lacking the muscle and killer good looks.

'And he already has a boyfriend,' Brad complained. 'Well, sort of. Ricky proudly just came out and told me he's a *kept man*. He lives with an older gentleman.'

'Nothing wrong with older gentlemen.' I grinned thinking about John.

'I know. But what if they also happen to be an escort?' Brad frowned and put the photo back in his wallet.

'An escort? You mean a prostitute?' I was about to laugh but realised Brad was serious. All I could say was, 'And you're still interested in this guy?'

'Oh yes. Ricky is super-hot. But we must practice safe sex because he's HIV positive. Ricky's incredible in bed!'

'Well of course if he's an escort. Brad, what are you getting yourself into? It sounds kind of messy!'

'I'm a big boy. I can handle it.'

In between working out with John at the gym and going to lectures, I began writing what I hoped to turn into a novel. I jotted down my observations of the gay scene into a notebook and typed up my thoughts eagerly in the Mac Lab. I also wrote a one-act play for the Creative Writing unit titled, 'The Psychiatrist'. It was largely autobiographical about my anger towards my parents for not understanding what it was like to hide a drug problem growing up. The Creative Writing lecturer, Karen Johnson, picked my play to be produced and videoed, a high honour as only 4 other students got their material filmed from 40.

In a casting decision that amused Brad to no end, Karen cast me to play the character based on myself because there was too much main character dialogue to remember unless one wrote it, of course. She cast John to play the psychiatrist and father figure. (I doubled up on characters to make the play cost efficient and multi-layered in terms of father figures). Doubling characters was a technique I learnt from studying the Australian playwriter Micheal Gow's play 'Away' in high school. To make things feel increasingly incestuous, Claire was cast to play the main character's drug addicted girl friend, a character based on Tiffany. Finally, Karen chose Matt to direct the play. Matt took on the task reluctantly. Since he hoped to direct movies one day, he accepted the opportunity, and finally talked to Claire and me for the first time in ages. All my love interests since starting university were on stage with me for an amateur re-interpretation of my life story. It was my first taste of art imitating life.

The dean of the faculty, Joseph, approached me after the play was screened and received applause. 'I enjoyed it!' Joseph sounded pleased. 'There was something in it that was captivating. You should write another act and get it up!' I grinned at Joseph's use of industry jargon.

The play was also well enjoyed by the other students, and I got a High Distinction for the Creative Writing subject.

By the time the spring mid-semester break rolled around, Brad and I were the first students onboard the XPT train bound for Central Station. Brad was counting down the hours until he got to see Ricky, while I looked forward to catching up with Dan. I was ready to see the guy I'd been thinking about ever since I left Sydney. I wanted to have a boyfriend my own age. I'd stopped having sex with John. It didn't compare to the heat I felt with Dan. I wanted to feel that spark again and be with the love of my life. My hopes were high.

I wasn't sure if Dan was that man, but he was a good start. What I wanted more than anything was to meet someone who'd always be there for me. Like John was there for Andy, minus the open relationship thing. No judgement, it just wasn't the way I was wired.

When I arrived in Sydney, I wasted no time looking up Dan. I phoned him the minute I got settled in my parents' home. 'Want to come out to play?' I asked coyly.

'Depends on what sort of game you have in mind.' I could hear the smile in Dan's voice.

That night, we met at The Albury Hotel. Dan gave me a polite kiss on the cheek, not the sort of kiss that said I missed you so much, more of a kiss that one gives to a friend. I didn't let this prevent me from throwing my arms around Dan to embrace him like he was a long-lost lover.

'Okay, I missed you too!' Dan chuckled in my ear. Then he took a closer look at me and commented, 'Have you been working out?' I was wearing a tight black Bonds t-shirt, and my bronzed biceps were on full display. After a few beers and conversation about what we'd been doing for the past several weeks, Dan held my hand as we walked towards the Oxford Hotel and then to the gayest of all gay clubs on Oxford Street, the Midnight Shift.

Because Dan held hands with me openly in pubic as we walked along Oxford Street, a group of men in a passing car yelled at us.

'Faggots!'

'Yes, that's true about both of us, nice of them to notice,' Dan said directly to me ignoring the name-callers.

Inside the safety of the Midnight Shift, I was reunited with Tiffany. She was seated in a booth with her arms around Mark. Tiffany made every head turn when she squealed at the sight of me entering the bar. I think I surprised her. I hadn't told her I was coming back to Sydney as I wanted to spend all my time with Dan.

Tiffany rushed over and threw her arms around me. 'Nathan, darling! I missed you so much! You look so handsome and strong! Have you got on the juice?'

'Juice?' I had no idea what Tiffany meant.

'Steroids!' Tiffany rolled her eyes as though I were stupid.

'No! These are all me.' I smiled proudly as Tiffany started rubbing and squeezing my biceps and chest pecs.

'Are you E'ing?' I grinned at Tiffany. It wasn't even midnight, and Tiffany was exuberantly altered with a giant grin as she was fixated on my physic.

'Benefits of dating a drug dealer.' Tiffany grinned as she chewed gum.

'Dating?' I enquired.

This was how I learnt Tiffany and Mark had become a drug-dealing power couple, moving illegal merchandise to half the patrons in the clubs

on Oxford Street, one of which I recalled from every time I'd been to DCM
– Dom. At the Midnight Shift, he danced on the giant Blackbox speaker. It
was like time had stood still on Oxford Street while I'd been away. Only the
music was new, Kathy Dennis 'Touch me (all night long)'.

After scoring from Tiffany's boyfriend, Dan took my hand and led me
into the middle of the dance floor. Under a cluster of mirror balls, flashing
lights, and men with their hands stretched up towards the DJ booth on the
side, Dan looked into my eyes. He smiled sweetly and moved in to steal a
gentle kiss. It had been so long since I felt so alive. My eyes beamed with
contentment as the E kicked in. The DJ played four Kylie Minogue songs in
a row from her 'Rhythm of love' album and the entire nightclub was cheering to; 'Better the devil you know', 'Step back in time', 'What do I have to
do?', and 'Shocked'. Dan and I danced with pure abandon. I was finally out
of the closet, and I was dancing in a gay club with a very cute and cool guy.
The man I hoped might become something more, if only we could get over
the temporary long-distance love thing.

'I'm turning twenty-one years old tomorrow,' Dan shouted in my ear.

'Happy birthday, Grandpa!' I yelled back.

'Hey, manners, young man! Respect your elders and all that shit!" Dan
laughed. "I'd like you to be at my party tomorrow night.'

'For sure!'

'That's what I was hoping.' Dan smiled.

On the opposite end of the dance floor, I spotted Brad dancing with
Ricky. Dan and I moved over to meet them.

Brad gave Dan a big hug and smiled. 'I was hoping you two would be
here!' Brad smiled. 'I'd like you to meet Ricky.'

Ricky wasn't listening and kept dancing. He seemed very out of it and
didn't look us in the eye. He kept dancing as we tried to get his attention.
However, Ricky's glassy eyes were fixed on the mirror balls and colourful
lights above. I couldn't tell if this was because Ricky was being rude or just
seriously off his face.

'Ricky, this is Dan and Nathan!' Brad shouted and grabbed Ricky's
shoulder with a gentle shake.

'Oh yeah. Hi!' Ricky smiled distantly and kept dancing.

For the next hour, we all danced within our chemical spells. Each of us had chosen to wear clothes that revealed our fit physiques. Collectively, our muscles were on display for the other boys in the club. I could tell we were being eyed-up by other men in the club as we danced. We danced with joy as we grooved to the beat of Marky Mark and the Funky Bunch's, 'Good vibrations'. I could feel we were the centre of attention for most of the men in the club that night, including Dom, who I caught watching us from his perch dancing above the crowd. I wondered if Dom was irritated that we were stealing focus from him.

By morning, Brad left to go home with Ricky.

That's when Dan told me he had to leave to go to work. I was disappointed to realise that what I'd been hoping for all night (getting into bed with Dan), wasn't going to happen at all. Reluctantly, I kissed and hugged Dan goodbye.

Suddenly, I was left alone on the thinning dance floor. The remaining men on the floor looked somewhat tragic. A few men gave me the eye, propositioning me like I was a desperate leftover. I quickly joined Tiffany and Mark in the booth.

'Want to come back to our place when this dive closes?' Mark asked.

'That's where the party will carry on!' Tiffany promised.

'Sure,' I agreed, not having anyone else to be with or anywhere else to go.

When the lights came on inside the Midnight Shift, everyone knew how messed up they looked as they scrambled for the exit. I followed Tiffany and Mark with a bunch of strangers to step outside into a new day.

Together, we stood with a group of several people I didn't know. Mark and Tiffany began walking up Oxford Street and a small crowd followed. We all stank of cigarette smoke and sweat. In the cool morning air, our clan passed a corner pub. Sitting outside the pub was a derelict man. The homeless man was sitting in a stupor of a methylated haze. His legs were spread apart, and his torso propped up against the locked door. He was too wasted to hold his head up to face us. Yet he lifted his right hand up to give us club kids a thumbs up as we floated by.

'Good morning, old chap!' Mark responded with a tone of respect. After being awake all night, we had mentally reached a point where we related to another old soul who was on a serious life-long bender. It was a fate that some of Mark's customers would no doubt face, I thought to myself absent-mindedly. I never thought for a second that becoming homeless could ever happen to me as I came down from MDMA. The rest of the clan followed Mark's good will and wished the derelict man, 'Good morning'.

In an odd way, I felt proud for greeting this homeless man and wondered why it took chemical assistance to give another human being respect, no matter who they were. I would have given the elderly man money too, if I'd had any. Being a student, I wasn't as financially solvent as Mark. In that instant, Mark gave the homeless man a fifty-dollar bill.

'Stay safe,' Mark said and continued to walk.

Mark was the Robin Hood of drug dealers. Dealing to the rich and giving to the homeless. The derelict man thanked Mark. He was in-tune with our collective state of mind, completely intoxicated, in a world where nothing made sense.

The walk back to Mark and Tiffany's home through the back streets of Surry Hills seemed to take forever. It didn't help that that we all had started to come down from the previous night's drugs.

'I need more speed!' Tiffany moaned before complaining she was too tired to go on. 'Mark, can you give me a piggyback?'

'Okay, darling.' Mark grinned as he let his stick-thin lover climb onto his broad shoulders.

'Does anyone know where we are?' one of Mark's customers asked.

'Admit it, Mark, we're no longer in Surry Hills, are we?' I joked.

'It's not that far!' Mark rolled his eyes. 'A few more blocks.'

With each terrace home that we passed, it felt like we had entered a new suburb.

'Passengers, we're passing through Strathfield, Campbelltown, Bankstown,' Tiffany copied the familiar Sydney train network announcement as we passed each home. I laughed and by the time we reached their apartment block on Flinders Street, Tiffany insisted we had reached 'Emu Plains', the last station on the Western Suburbs train line.

It was such a relief to enter the silence of the empty apartment. The soothing neutral grey and beige colour scheme of the walls, carpet, and furniture helped ease the comedown and softened the hallucinations, other than the sound of a low hum ringing in my ears, the usual side effect of dancing for too long under the speakers. The apartment was quiet and felt safe.

Our next activity involved laying on the carpet and passing around a skull-shaped bong packed with dope. All eight of the disorientated clubbers Mark had invited to his apartment recovered by inhaling marijuana smoke. Even though I didn't know any of the other people, this didn't stop me from happily joining them for breakfast with another ecstasy pill to start the day. Unlike the rest, mine was free from Tiffany, compliments from her drug dealing boyfriend. She even offered me to have a hot shower and get changed into some comfy gear as Mark and I were the same size. Once I returned to the living room in Eastern Suburbs National Rugby League Roosters shorts and jersey, Tiffany announced, 'Breakfast is the most important meal of the day!' as she handed me the speckled pill.

'Eccie for breakie!' I grinned.

The front door opened, and more people arrived in the living room. To my surprise, Tiffany and Mark's other roommate turned out to be Dom, the self-appointed Dancing Adonis. He'd finally vacated his podium. Dom burst into the apartment with another group of strangers.

'What's happening, bitches?' Dom grabbed the bong. He seemed to know everyone in the living room except me. After being introduced by Tiffany, Dom pretty much ignored me as morning slid into midday. Instead of talking, Dom and I played a silent drug-fucked mind game of looking at each other but not saying a word. Until Dom unexpectedly pointed out in admiration, 'Look how brown your legs are, Nathan!' In that instant, I regretted my earlier decision to slip into a pair of Mark's rugby shorts to get out of my stinky club clothes. Dom's remark drew everyone's attention to my legs. The hallucinating club kids agreed with enthusiasm at how brown my sexy, muscular legs were.

For months, I had done as John advised and made sure I included calf muscles in my exercise routine. Plus, the gym's solarium made my skin golden brown. Dressed in Mark's Roosters National Rugby League jersey and shorts, I looked like a young, intoxicated star football recruit. The club kids began rubbing their hands over my legs. I grew self-conscious, feeling like a house pet as strangers took turns stroking me. At the same time, I noticed how porcelain white some of Mark, Tiffany, and Dom's friends' skin was. Suddenly, I felt as though I was hanging out with a bunch of vampires and had retired to their crypt the morning after a night of feeding. It looked like two had not seen the light of day for a year or so. Had they been club-bing for that long?

'Wow. How'd you get such a great tan?' one of them asked in all seri-ousness.

'My bronzed skin is thanks to me studying so close to Byron Bay,' I informed the club kids. 'The hole in the ozone layer has made it permanently summer up north.'

All my new underground mates giggled at my observation. It dawned on me how much healthier I looked than Mark and Tiffany's customers. No longer under the disco lights, but in the light of day, the goth couple I noticed earlier looked like gravely ill hospital patients with bluish white skin, each being propped-up by an assortment of illegal chemicals that con-tained God knows what.

WANT TO BE MY BOYFRIEND?

'THIS PARTY IS so pretentious!' Tiffany complained within ten minutes of arriving at Dan's twenty-first birthday party. The party was at a grand old terrace on Bayswater Road, in Kings Cross. The large living room was filled with people Dan knew from what he described as '*Sydney's A-list*'. He explained the crowd consisted of individuals from the arts scene, fashion scene, journalism industry, Sydney university, and hangers-on. He then excused himself because he had to *meet and greet,* leaving Tiffany and I alone to observe a room full of strangers.

'It's not really our scene, is it?' I had to agree with Tiffany.

'The crowd is so cold,' Tiffany folded her arms.

'Wait till their drugs kick in,' I offered. I did feel out of place with so many unapproachable people in the room. I wondered if it was because I went to a country university rather than a city one, or rather if the crowd were simply a bunch of snobs.

'Let's get a drink,' Tiffany suggested.

We headed towards a make-shift bar by the windows. Behind the table was a barman dressed in a black and white suit with a bowtie.

'What'll it be?' The barman asked. Tiffany ordered a gin and tonic, as did I. Dan was in the opposite corner with Brad. They were comforting Stevie, who was getting emotionally psyched up to do his first public drag performance. Dan noticed me watching from across the room and gave me a wink and a smile. The small gesture warmed my heart.

'Let's split and go to DCM!' Tiffany pleaded. 'We can get free Es and have some fun.'

'I can't leave Dan on his twenty-first birthday.'

'There are heaps of people here to help him celebrate.' Tiffany downed her gin and tonic. 'Tell him you'll meet him later at The Taxi Club when the party's over. This party is full of such uptight wannabes.'

'But, Tiffany, I really like Dan.'

'Then why isn't Dan hanging out with you?'

I didn't have an answer for that, other than he was distracted with so many of his friends in the one room. The only other person I knew at the party was Brad, and he was being introduced to Ricky's friends, who were all older gentlemen, probably clients. I hoped *Brad wasn't being sold!* I thought for split-second. The older men were all dressed in the most expensive designer clothes, wearing suit jackets and acting so superior.

When Dan approached me, he looked very happy and kissed me on the lips. He was holding a glass of champagne. 'Thanks for coming!'

'Happy Birthday, babe!' I smiled. "Cheers!" Dan and I clinked our glasses wearing loving smiles.

'Dan we're going to leave now for DCM. You know how it is; we've got friends to meet,' Tiffany blurted out abruptly.

Dan seemed taken aback but pretended to understand. 'Oh, yeah that's fine. I get it, you're on your break and you want to be on the dance floor, not here with us boring old farts.'

'Do you want to meet up at The Taxi Club later when this wraps up?' I asked Dan, hoping he wouldn't meet someone new at his party.

'Sure, we'll be there eventually. But who knows what state we'll be in!'

'Us too!' Tiffany winked.

We stayed at Dan's party long enough to witness Stevie perform '*Happy Birthday, Mr President*', but he changed the word 'President' to Dan's surname 'Masterson'. Tiffany and I fled the party as the crowd cheered 'More!' and 'Encore!'. After fleeing Dan's twenty-first, I walked with Tiffany along Darlinghurst Road towards Taylor Square.

'I'm glad we're friends again!' Tiffany confessed.

'Me too,' I agreed, although, secretly, I felt annoyed she'd made me leave the party. What if Dan met someone else!

'Who else would save you from dud parties like that?' Tiffany joked.

'I think there was more to it, right?'

'Okay, I admit it. I need to be at DCM to keep an eye on Mark. He needs me to keep an eye out for undercover cops. Plus, I need to ward off all the fag hags trying to make a move on my man!'

'Or some man?' I smirked.

'No. Mark's already been there and tried that. It wasn't for him.'

'Really?'

'Wasn't for him. Mark and Dom hooked up a few times when they were younger and in high school.'

'Your roommate? That big guy!'

'The Vogue dancer, yes!' Tiffany confirmed with a big grin. 'Dom and Mark fooled around.'

'For real?' I was amazed at this revelation. 'Details, please!'

'Mark said they experimented in high school more than once when they used to get stoned, but Mark grew out of it. Dom never did. Dom still teases Mark, saying he's in denial. Dom said I need to watch that one!'

'He's probably right! After all, they still live together!' I warned Tiffany and thought about my one-off fooling around with Matt in Lismore. My mind was filled with questions. I wanted to know more, like how far Dom and Mark had gone with each other. Was Dom any good? I pondered. And if Dom was good, why would Mark be with a girl now? Unless of course Mark was like me a several months ago, secretly gay and dating a girl to pretend he was heterosexual. Or he could even be bisexual. The 90s were full of possibilities.

I didn't want to think about the possibility Mark could be like Matt in Lismore, a straight-acting guy who had no problem doing boys on the side, provided it was kept secret, but who would kill anyone if they ever told.

Just as we'd done when we used to go to The Exchange Hotel when we were underage, Tiffany and I waltzed past the *tragedies* lining up hoping to get into DCM. Tiffany grinned at the bouncer, and he nodded for us to enter, no questions asked. The bouncer knew Tiffany was the drug dealer's girlfriend, a VIP, with me as a plus-one, a VIP by association.

In the bar, Tiffany found Mark in his usual position, selling Es and speed from the back booth. He was sandwiched between two girls still hanging around from the previous morning.

'Moles!' Tiffany said under her breath before she kissed each girl hello, just like they were best friends. Tiffany pushed her way in between the moles and her man. 'How's business tonight, babe?'

'Booming. Sold out! Ready to head home.' Mark grinned and flashed a wad of cash under the cover of the table. 'Look what I saved for you, my love.' Mark pulled out a satchel containing two pills. Tiffany took hers and loudly offered me the other one.

'Nathan!' Tiffany yelled to grab my attention, as I'd taken to watching Dom dancing on the podium. It was quite a compelling sight.

'Do they pay him to do that?' I asked.

'Why would they?' Mark laughed. 'When he does it for free?'

Tiffany grabbed my hand. 'Babe, priorities.' She handed me a pill. 'It's either an upper or a downer.' Tiffany joked. 'It will make you feel fabulous!'

'Thanks, hon.' I smiled and took the pill without a second thought.

From the corner booth, my gaze remained glued to Dom's dancing silhouette cutting through the beaming green laser lights. After an hour of dancing non-stop, Dom hopped off the podium, drenched in sweat. He was puffing hard and placed his hands on his waist like an athlete recovering from a marathon. Dom took a sip of water from a bottle on the table as he continued to perspire.

It was at this moment I felt the effects of the pill that Tiffany gave me kick in. I left the booth to dance by the edge of the packed dance floor. It was like another world, full of the most wonderful people dancing in time to KLF's, '3 a.m. Eternal'.

The lasers and flashing lights played pleasant tricks with my eyes. One was the image of Dom standing by my side. At first, I thought it was a hallucination, until I realised it really was Dom standing there. Standing side by side, I was dwarfed by Dom's muscular physique. He was a huge man compared to me, much taller and broader.

'Want to do a line of speed?' Dom yelled in my ear.

'Sure!' I was never one to refuse the offer of free drugs from a virtual stranger. Being a student meant I had zero money to spend on luxuries. I followed Dom through the crowded club towards the female toilets upstairs.

The *Ladies* bathroom was busy with both guys and girls waiting for one of the three cubicles to become free.

As the mob waited, the muffled sounds of music from the dance floor below was interrupted by occasional loud snorting sounds coming from behind the closed doors. Dom didn't make any conversation; he kept smiling at me and I couldn't help but smile back.

It felt like a weird dream, surreal, as each breath tingled. I didn't know what to say and just melted into the tiled wall as the E engulfed my central nervous system. My heart raced not just from the MDMA but from a sense of excitement at being alone with Dancing Dom. Dom continued to sweat profusely from the performance he had just given on the podium and the illicit chemicals in his system.

'I love the way you dance!' A girl waiting ahead of us in the queue smiled at Dom.

'Oh, thanks, love!' Dom was visibly flattered by the compliment.

Two toilet cubicle doors opened at the same time, and four people exited. No one was going to the bathroom to expel waste, but rather to inhale what they hoped would be uppers. Also, when you live on chemicals, you have nothing to expel, I thought with amusement as I followed Dom into the empty cubicle.

With the door shut and the lock switched from *Vacant* to *Engaged*, Dom pulled a plastic satchel containing a white crystalised powder from his black pants. He kneeled and emptied the powder onto the back of the black toilet seat lid. Dom chopped up four lines of speed with a credit card, then rolled up a fifty-dollar note, and took a snort. As I watched Dom kneeling over the night club toilet seat, I wondered if Tiffany was right about *blasting speed* being cleaner than snorting it, especially compared to inhaling it off a dingy night club toilet seat lid. Who knew what was being sniffed? Being a dedicated club kid wasn't all glamour.

Dom was such a big man there was barely any room left in the tight cubicle for me to stand as I watched, squashed into the corner. Dom handed me the rolled-up note. 'Your turn,' he finally spoke.

I bent down and did the same and soon felt a familiar sting down my nasal cavity and the back of my throat. Once I finished inhaling the lines, Dom and I stood facing each other. I was waiting for Dom to unlock the cubicle door, but instead was taken off-guard when he suddenly thrust forward, pressed his body against mine and planted his lips on my lips. His tongue was deep in my mouth touching my tongue. As Dom kissed me aggressively, I was taken by surprise, flattered by this form of attention being unleashed on me. I thought Dom was attractive but had had no idea that he was even remotely interested in me.

Once Dom was done, he pulled back and looked pleased with himself. 'I think you're cute!' He grinned with his dilated pupils staring into my dilated pupils.

'I think you're a good dancer!' I smiled, feeling like what I just said was stupid. I was still startled and excited by what was happening.

'Want to be my boyfriend?' Dom asked enthusiastically.

'Yes!' I agreed over enthusiastically high on the love drug and a few lines of speed. 'I totally want to be your boyfriend!' I responded. Having a *boyfriend* was on the top of my priority list. It was the one thing I wanted most in the world, and being chemically altered, I felt intensely happy with this turn of events. It was finally happening, I thought with joy. I had a boyfriend! I'd met Mr Right.

I was feeling so inexplicably excited at having scored a boyfriend in the toilets of DCM that I forgot all about my original plan to meet my other potential romance, Dan, later at The Taxi Club.

The amphetamines were increasing the intensity of every emotion until my mind turned to thoughts of Dan. What would I tell Dan? Then I realised The Taxi Club was somewhere in the future. All that mattered was the present, what was happening right here, right now. Maybe Dan, Dom, and I could have an open relationship like John and Andy, or be as Dan once joked, 'One big incestuous family'.

I was so off my face I had no idea what I was doing, or who I was doing it with. All that mattered was what was feeling good and being in the moment. Reality and tomorrow were miles away.

As my new boyfriend, Dom and I exited the toilet cubicle. We held hands and were both grinning from ear to ear. We still had little to say to each other, until Dom announced the news to the mob seated in the back booth with Tiffany and Mark. 'Hey everyone, we're boyfriends!' Dom yelled.

'Yay!' Tiffany squealed.

'Congrats, boys!' Mark nodded.

The assortment of club kids around the booth, were ecstatic at this news. After all, they were also all high on illicit substances supplied by Mark. Each of the hangers-on congratulated Dom for making me his *new boyfriend.*

'He's really cute,' I heard one say.

'I'm really happy for you, Nathan!' Tiffany yelled in my ear and gave me a hug. 'Do you see why I wanted to get you out of that lame twenty-first party. I knew Dom liked you heaps!'

'So does Dan!' I was starting to have second thoughts about how fast and chaotic this chain of events was. To make matters worse, the next thing Mark said also reminded me of Dan.

'Welcome to the family, sweetheart!' Mark shook my hand in a very formal way.

'Oh my God!' Tiffany exclaimed at the song the DJ started to play. It was Alison Limerick's, 'Where love lives'. 'Dom and Nathan, this is your song!' Tiffany grinned from ear to ear as she gave us both big, tight, ecstasy induced embrace.

I began to dance with my drug induced boyfriend and his friends as Alison's deep vocals sang about going down, deep down, where love lives. I looked at Dom, who was grinning from ear to ear. Dom looked so pleased with himself. Extremely happy and staring into my eyes with pure contentment.

'I love you so much!' Dom told me with complete sincerity.

I didn't care if it was just the MDMA talking. 'I love you too!' I responded, feeling on top of the world. It all felt so real, so exciting, so meant to be.

Later, in the early hours at The Taxi Club, I still felt incredibly happy yet suddenly awkward the minute Dan arrived with Brad, Ricky, Emma, and Stevie (who was still in drag). At first, Dan was happy at the sight of me, but he looked puzzled instantly when he noticed Dom's hands were wrapped around my waist.

'Dan, this is Dom!' I introduced my two love interests to one another. Before I had a chance to explain what happened, Dom announced the good news.

'I'm Nathan's boyfriend!'

Dan's eyes widened and his brow rose at the revelation with pure confusion. 'Boyfriend?' Dan repeated, a mixture of intoxication and disappointment. 'Boyfriend! Nathan, you didn't tell me Dom was your boyfriend.'

I looked towards my Doc Martin boots on the messed-up dance floor for comfort. Even on drugs, I sensed what I had just allowed to happen wasn't the twenty-first birthday present Dan had been hoping for. I also felt confused through the haze of amphetamines. It was Dan I'd originally hoped to end up with by night's end, until I took a free E, and accepted a kind offer to snort lines of speed with a stranger.

'It just happened at DCM.' I shrugged, drugs fading, reality setting in.

'In the lady's toilets!' Dom added with a chuckle.

I witnessed the disappointment flash across Dan's face. I couldn't help but consider the possibility that it was happening again. I was making questionable decisions while high, just like when I was a sixteen-year-old. At nineteen-years-old, I still couldn't handle my drugs. The whole reason I went to Lismore was to avoid this type of situation and scene. In the moment that followed I realised what a class act Dan really was.

'Congratulations. I'm really, happy for you both, really,' Dan managed to say calmly, but through a clenched smile. It was the last thing Dan said to me that night as he regrouped with Brad, Ricky, Emma, and Stevie who was now out-of-drag and looked somewhat androgynous. I could tell they were gossiping about what had just happened as I danced with Dom on the tiny dance floor. Dan and Brad's friends spent the last few hours of the night pretending I didn't exist and soon left without saying goodbye.

I danced with my new boyfriend, feeling unsure about what had happened. I discovered all it took was one free pill and a generous gift of two lines of speed to leave one big incestuous family for another.

I hoped I'd made the right decision as I watched the man I picked to be my Mr Right dance energetically by my side in The Taxi Club. I could tell he was annoying other patrons for dancing so wildly and they literally had to move out of Dom's way to avoid getting struck. Dom took up a large space in the middle of the tiny dance floor and from the way he danced, he acted like he owned the club. Dancing Dom was riding high. He danced like I wasn't even dancing right next to him. His limbs were swinging in all directions, and inevitably ended up whacking me right on my neck.

'Sorry, baby!' Dom broke from his dance trance to cuddle me sooth-ingly. 'Are you okay?'

"I'm okay, babe," I answered, disorientated and with a throbbing Adam apple from where I'd been struck. Love struck me hard on the love drug.

SAFE SEX

THE MORNING AFTER, I couldn't wait to go to bed with Dom. Unfortunately, so was Tiffany. As Dom and I found ourselves naked and under the covers about to kiss, Tiffany burst into Dom's bedroom and jumped under the doona cover with us. Tiffany giggled, knowing she was invading our private space but didn't seem to care. She was elated, not just from her third ecstasy pill for the night, but because her two most favourite men in the world were now boyfriends.

'I couldn't have planned it better!' Tiffany bragged, clapping her hands enthusiastically.

'It's meant to be!' Dom agreed as he held me tight.

'I still can't believe it!' I agreed.

'You make such a handsome couple!' Tiffany smiled.

I was dying for our uninvited bedroom gate crasher to get out of the queen-sized bed and leave me alone with Dom. I was so horny that I couldn't control my right hand from feeling Dom's enormous penis under the covers, even while Tiffany bounced on his other side of the bed.

'You're both so cute and good looking!' Tiffany rambled, completely elated. 'And you're both such good dancers and–'

'Love, we're beat!' Dom gave Tiffany the hint she needed to leave us alone.

'And I want to consummate our relationship!' I laughed.

'Time we all got some shut-eye.' Dom winked.

'Oh…yes. I'm *really* tired too!' Tiffany winked back. 'I promise I won't hear a thing! Have fun, boys. But I want all the details when you wake up!'

With Tiffany gone and the door closed, Dom kissed me softly on the lips. We could feel each other's erections pressed against one another. The sensation and heat from Dom's rock-hard cock filled me with desire. It was the first time I was ready to let another man go all the way with me. My heart raced as Dom's hand moved down my belly to grab hold of my dick.

But suddenly Dom pulled his hand away. 'I don't want this to be just another one-night stand.' Dom broke our kiss to look in my eyes.

'Me neither!' I was touched by Dom's words. 'I want you to be my boyfriend forever! For life I mean!'

'Me too!' Dom sounded pleasantly surprised. 'That's why I don't think we should fuck straight away. I want to get to know you properly first.'

'Huh?'

'Let's just stay in each other's arms and talk.'

'I'm horny as hell, aren't you?'

'Yes. But I really, *really* want to get to know you first. I don't want this to turn out to be just another one-night stand.' What Dom said impressed me, it also frustrated me. Dom was the first man I had met who didn't just want to get straight to sex. It seemed so old fashioned. What Dom was proposing was unusual for a gay man in the 90s. I was equal parts flattered and bitterly disappointed. I found the remaining hours of the morning pressed against Dom's large body, kissing and talking intimately a kind of torture. It was impossible to concentrate on the questions Dom was asking.

'How old are you?'

'What do you do?'

'Where are you from?'

'How many boyfriends have you had?'

All I could think about was what it would be like to get off with Dom. But instead, I had to settle for having an endless conversation. It was a very one-way conversation, where Dom did all the talking, mainly about himself. I quickly learnt Dom had a high opinion of himself. Dom was twenty-one-years-old. He'd grown up on the North Shore, worked as a personal banker, and was once engaged to a high school sweetheart, Monica, but he broke it off when he came out just a year ago. Coming down from ecstasy, it started to annoy me the way Dom couldn't stop talking about himself.

Why delay the inevitable? I was nineteen-years old and interested in one thing. I thought being *gay* meant having a license and the freedom to hook-up, and having sex provided you used a condom and kept it safe. To me, being gay was about liberated men having sex with other liberated men. What was there to discuss?

'I really think you're special. I want us to be together for a long time. I'm sick of the gay scene and all those guys who are out for just one thing,' Dom said as morning slipped into midday. 'They think just because I can dance, I can fuck like a maniac in the sack.'

'Admittedly, I can't wait to find out if that's true myself!' I gave Dom a cheeky grin. 'I suspect you can.'

'You're too cute. I wish we could stay like this forever.' Dom rolled on top of me.

Finally, some action my heart swelled with excitement. 'Me too!' I felt like I was in a strange dream.

We cuddled and fell asleep from sleep deprivation.

~

The next day, Tiffany and I went shopping for condoms and lubricant at the Tool Shed on Oxford Street. This was in preparation for my next date with Dom.

'So, you just kissed and cuddled?' Tiffany was utterly surprised at this revelation.

'Dom is an old-fashioned kind of guy,' I replied.

'No, he's not! Dom's a slut!' Tiffany shook her head dismissively. 'I should know. We share a common wall.'

'A slut?'

'Big time! Dom must be serious about you not to go all the way on your first time.'

Once inside the adult concepts store, we couldn't help but burst into laughter at the sight of a glass cabinet display lined with enormous dildos. The sex toys came in all sizes imaginable. There were two other men in the store. A lone man looked at covers of pornographic videocassettes and another attractive younger man was behind the cash register.

I headed for the counter containing the lube and condoms. 'So, what should I go for?' I grinned pointing at a range of lubricants that came in an assortment of fruit flavours. 'Banana, strawberry, or apple?'

'Banana,' Tiffany instructed.

It was the first time I'd bought condoms or lube. 'What colour do I get?' I asked Tiffany as I considered the options, black, clear and ripped for pleasure.

'I like clear ones.' Tiffany shrugged.

'I can't believe we're doing this!'

'Yep, we're all grown up now and shopping in a sex store! Welcome to love in the 90s!' Tiffany smiled. 'I'm glad to know you're being sensible, Nathan. These days, you've got to play safe, especially with a guy who has had as any many roots as Dom!'

I grew uneasy at what Tiffany said. 'Just how many partners are you talking about?'

'Let's just say Dom's *danced* with most of the boys at DCM.'

'So, it's not me he really likes, it's just that he's been through all the men at DCM?'

'Perhaps?' Tiffany's brow raised. 'No, don't be ridiculous. Dom's really into you. He couldn't stop talking about how hot you looked dressed as a NRL player.'

'I know, because I was such a sporty kid.' I said full of sarcasm with my psychological scars from being called faggot and poofter during my days in physical education class at high school.

Tiffany burst out laughing loudly, disturbing the store's only other customer. He jumped nervously. 'Now for the more important question,' Tiffany sounded serious suddenly. 'When it comes to condoms, what size? I think I know the answer already.'

'From what I felt the other morning, Dom's going to need extra-large!'

'I knew it!' Tiffany did a little dance and laughed.

The following night on our first proper date, I came to realise that Dom was the type of guy who was persuasive and got exactly what he wanted. Without the love drug making him puppy-eyed, this night, there was nothing holding Dom back. After having dinner at Café 191 at Taylor Square, the next thing on the menu was Dom's convincing me to sit on his dick.

'I've never done that with anyone before!' I admitted awkwardly now completely sober.

'Show me how much you love me!' Dom urged.

'Dom I'm not making this up. I'm a virgin in that way.'

'You'll love it,' Dom said reassuringly.

In the dark, feeling both aroused and anxious I told myself that it was time I found out what it was like. I hoped it would feel better than that one time I tried it with John. In my heart, I knew Dom was the perfect guy to do it with. But at the same time, I was also scared of what we were about to do. What if it hurt? I was particularly anxious because Dom had an even bigger penis than John. But what alarmed me most was the sight up of Dom lubricating his cock without putting a condom on it first.

'What about the condom?' I asked.

'Just try sitting on it,' Dom said in a soothing voice. By this stage, I was so horny and desperate to have sex with Dom that I was ready to do just about anything he suggested. But not this.

'No. Let's use a condom!' I insisted.

'I don't like them,' Dom smiled like it wasn't a big deal.

'Come on, Dom!' I protested. 'We've only just met.'

'Seriously, it will be fine Nathan. I don't have AIDS. I'm one hundred percent certain you don't!' Dom grinned.

I paused, horny and unsure what to do next. 'I trust you!'

Dom tried to reassure me. 'It'll be okay.'

I positioned the tip of Dom's erection against my bare butt and carefully lowered my body onto him. But it only took a second before I cried out in pain. 'Fuck! No way Dom. Can't do it!' I hopped off the bed, then paced back and forth to shake the pain away as I continued to feel the sting.

Dom cracked up, laughing. 'Just breath, and it will be fine.'

I returned to the bed, took a deep breath, and tried to let Dom enter me. 'Ouch! Seriously, I can't do it!' I said, disappointed. Once again, there was too much pain to handle.

'Ok, why don't you fuck me?' Dom shrugged.

I was taken back by this suggestion. Dom was such a big guy compared to me that it never occurred to me that I would be topping him. I reached for the condom wrapper when Dom grabbed my hand.

'We don't need that.' Dom shrugged.

'Of course, we do!' I insisted.

'I want to feel you inside me,' Dom crooned.

I felt alarmed and hesitant at the thought of having sex without a condom. Doing so went against my better judgment, and everything I'd been taught growing up during the AIDS epidemic of the 80s. But on this night, common sense was overridden by my intense desire to have sex with Dom. He was obviously a risk taker, seducing inexperienced guys like me in the DCM toilets and later insisting on unsafe sex in his bedroom.

I wet my dick with the banana flavoured lubricant. I felt stupid about buying condoms I wasn't even going to use. The feeling of stupidity was soon overridden by the intense pleasure of sliding into Dom. Despite the pleasure, the whole experience was not as I imagined it would be. My first time inside another man without protection felt hotter and more intense than it had felt with John. Except, with each thrust, my paranoia grew. I couldn't stop the creeping feeling I was making a massive mistake having unsafe sex with a man I barely knew, a man who my best friend described as *'a slut'*.

As I climaxed inside Dom, for a split second, I reminded myself how easy it was to catch HIV by having unsafe sex just once. As I experienced incredible pleasure, I was experiencing debilitating fear, knowing I could be willingly exposing myself to HIV. Afterwards, we lay in each other's arms, breathing heavily. I recognised with growing unease, just how much I was prepared to risk for what I thought would turn into real love. Fresh out of high school, a first-year university student who'd recently come out, I was prepared to do anything to have a partner in life.

I was an easy target for someone more experienced.

'That was the greatest fuck I've ever had!' Dom complimented me, sounding amazed.

'Incredible!' I agreed riddled with instant regret. 'You do fuck as you dance. You're a maniac in the sack.'

OUTED

THE REMAINING DAYS of spring break were spent living at Dom's apartment in Surry Hills. By day while Dom worked, I joined Tiffany with her band in their home recording studio. I loved watching Tiffany lay down vocals as she smoked joints.

'Your songs are awesome!' I complimented Tiffany and her band. Their music sounded like it was produced by a European DJ. I liked their song 'Illegal glamour' the best.

During the evenings, back at the apartment, Mark's customers came and went. They purchased ecstasy, trips, and speed. I was amazed to hear the security intercom buzz every fifteen minutes. Each time Mark opened the front door, it revealed another familiar face or two from DCM, Midnight Shift, or The Taxi Club crowd.

People from all walks of life entered the apartment eager to buy disco biscuits, small plastic satchels of white crystals full of illicit substances in preparation for the weekend. Or weekday, who knew? Due to Mark's line of business, it was like my new boyfriend and ex-girlfriend knew everyone who was anyone on the scene.

After several days of not returning to my parents' home to eat or sleep or even get change of fresh clothes, I phoned my mum to let her know I was okay and was not dead. When I dialled my parents, it was with the intention of letting mum know I'd be coming home tomorrow to see her. I had to pack my bags for another stretch of university in Lismore.

'Hello?'

'Hi, Mum. Sorry I haven't been around much. I've been staying at Tiffany's–' I started until my mum cut me off mid-sentence.

'Nathan, I've told your father.'

'Told him what?'

'I had to tell him why you were spending all your time in Surry Hills. He was getting suspicious.'

'Suspicious?'

'I told him you're a *gay*.'

My heart skipped a beat. There was a pause as I processed this. 'What did he say?'

'Not much.' Mum sounded aloof. 'He seemed a bit disappointed.'

I didn't know what to say. I was disappointed to hear that my father's reaction to me being gay was *disappointment*. Suddenly, I grew scared of facing dad before returning to university, fear of being financially cut off filled my soul.

At the same time, I was glad my mum had broken the news to my dad. It was long overdue. There was a strange sense of relief, although I was annoyed mum had robbed me of the opportunity to tell dad, in my own words, that I was gay. The realisation hit me that I had nothing left to hide from my parents, apart from the fact my new boyfriend lived with a drug dealer.

'Okay,' I said after an awkward silence. 'I'll be home tomorrow, so I will see you both then.'

'Okay. I just wanted you to know I told him, that's all. Bye.' Mum hung up without waiting for me to say *bye*. She was unusually short with me. I guess she was still upset that I came out. That I was growing up and becoming a young adult who was out and proud.

Dom looked concerned at my expression of dismay. 'What is it?' Dom asked cautiously.

'Fucking hell!' I ran my fingers through my thick hair. 'My mum just told my dad I'm gay. She outed me!'

'Bullshit! How did he take it?'

'Disappointed.'

'That's better than being disowned like me.'

'Were you disowned?' I asked Dom apprehensively.

'Long story,' Dom said dismissively. 'Don't think now is the time to tell you how it went down.'

~∽

I timed the return to my parents' home so that it would be as brief as possible. It was Sunday, ninety minutes before I needed to catch the XPT Train back to Lismore. My plan was to pack my bags as quickly as possible before getting on board the train bound for Lismore. As I entered my parent's home, I honestly did not know what to expect knowing Mum had told Dad I was *'a gay'*.

The negative voice in my head spoke up, saying things like, *'Now you've done it! Dad's going to disown you!'*

"I'm home!" I called out as I opened the front door. I felt nervous. I was wearing Mark's clubbing clothes, sporting the light reflecting fabric of a Surry Hill drug dealer.

"Hello, Nathan!" Mum replied from the living room upon hearing my voice.

There was nothing said from my father.

I took a step inside to the living room fearing the worst.

On the TV, the film 'Calamity Jane' was playing. It was mum's favourite Doris Day movie. She was ironing and watching the movie play in the background. Mum and I had watched 'Calamity Jane' many times together when I was growing up. We both loved to watch any Doris Day film together. Mum had said that 'Calamity Jane' was the first film she'd ever seen at a cinema in Dalby Queensland when she was twelve years old, when she had been a little girl with her classmates. Her parents had had to sign a permission slip so she could see it with her school friends. Mum said she'd thought that 'Calamity Jane' was the best thing ever. I wondered if she'd ever noticed the lesbian subtext of this film, or was she blind to it?

Dad was seated in the armchair reading The Sydney Morning Herald broadsheet newspaper. He looked up at me and didn't say a thing.

"Hi, Dad!" I sat next to Mum on the sofa as Doris Day sang, 'My secret Love'. I grinned as Doris sang about how her secret love wasn't a secret anymore. I knew how Doris felt!

Now everything was incredibly awkward because no one was prepared to say a word for what seemed like an uncomfortably long time as we listened to the words of the song. It was up to me to break the silence. I turned to my father and said, "Mum said she told you I'm gay."

"Yes," Dad didn't move his gaze from the newspaper to look at me. Then he looked up at me, "I always knew there was something wrong with you when you dressed up as Boy George from Culture Club when you were a kid."

I had to suppress the sudden urge to laugh at this observation. I was almost hyperventilating, trying not to giggle for a second. I think I was still a little high from a week of amphetamines. Regardless, I was annoyed Dad thought there was something *"wrong"* with me for being *"a gay"*, and I didn't want to start an argument by making a big deal about this. I didn't want to give Dad an excuse to disapprove any further or disown me, as other less enlightened parents such as Dom's had done. I spoke from the heart, 'I'm glad you know, Dad. I wanted to tell you so many times, but I was afraid.'

'Nathan, I think I always knew!' Dad surprised me with this comment and looked at me with a half-smile. Wasn't it meant to be mothers who always knew? 'What the hell are you wearing, Nathan?' Dad asked curiously. 'You look like you're dressed to go into outer space, not a country town.'

Mark's clothes were cutting-edge early 90s clubbing fashion inspired, very futuristic, flashy and shiny, not a natural fibre on me. I was out, proud, and dressed like a gay robot sent back in time from the future to warn my parents I was queer. It was the perfect outfit that screamed, I'm here, I'm queer, get used to it!

Later that afternoon from the Central Station train platform, Dom and Tiffany waved goodbye from outside the XPT train carriage window. This was after Dom, and I caused something of a public scandal on the platform by openly kissing and hugging each other goodbye. We brazenly kissed each other as passionately as any heterosexual couple would. In response to our expression of love, a mother covered her young son's eyes at the sight of two men embracing. I felt somewhat self-conscious.

Tiffany smiled when it came her turn to hug me goodbye. 'I'm going to miss you, gorgeous!' She smiled warmly.

'Me too!' I confessed. 'It's going to be so much harder to be away now.' I looked into Dom's eyes.

All I wanted to do was be with Dom. University and preparing for my future career was now an inconvenience. I was head over heels in love. Tiffany was right, I now completely regretted my decision to study in a country town away from home. I hadn't counted on the possibility of falling in love, or the prospect of having a long-distance relationship.

As the train moved away from the station, I smiled as Tiffany and Dom ran along the platform trying to keep up with the moving train, just like people did in old Hollywood movies. I mouthed the words *'Love you'*, to Dom before he disappeared out of view.

I found myself feeling alone sitting in a packed carriage bound for Lismore. I had to transfer to a Sydney university. Either that or drop out. Forget about the illicit substances Mark sold, it was Dom that I'd become addicted to. In such a short time, I felt I couldn't live without him. I wrote my thoughts and feelings down in a diary as the train sped through the countryside.

Back in Lismore, I wasted no time preparing an application to transfer to the BA Communication course at the University of Technology Sydney (UTS). The only thing on my mind was to be closer to my boyfriend. This motivation had a strong influence over how I answered tedious questions on the application form. For instance, in response to the question, 'Who are your major influences?' I wrote *'ABBA, Madonna, Brett Easton Ellis's – 'Less than zero', Lee Tulloch's 'Fabulous Nobodies' and my boyfriend. Which is the real reason why I want to transfer to UTS.'*

I hoped honesty was the best approach to apply for a placement at the most prestigious humanities degree in Australia. I took an honestly humanitarian approach on my application. I pleaded to the institution to bring me closer to my boyfriend and complete a degree.

'I can't believe you chose that awful, pretentious, ridiculous queen over Dan!' Brad scolded me as soon as he saw me for the first time since our last encounter at The Taxi Club. Now we were seated opposite each other at the university café.

'Well, I can't believe you're with a prostitute!' I fired back about Brad's interest in Ricky.

'You know none of us can stand that guy! He's a complete narcissist,' Brad ignored my comeback and kept up his attack. "Dom is vile! You're embarrassing yourself by being seen in public with him!'

'I don't care what you say Brad,' I said flatly. 'I've fallen in love with him.'

'Oh please!' Brad scoffed. 'I'm sure it is just the drugs that made you think that. What were you on when you met Dom? E? Surely, by now you know MDMA makes you think you love just about anyone. Just wait till the drugs are out of your system and you realise what a serious mistake you've made! Dan was heartbroken, by the way! You could search the world twice and still never find a better guy to be with than Dan!'

'I never meant to hurt Dan,' I paused as Brad's words sunk in. I felt my heart sink at Brad's revelation. I hadn't taken the time to think about how Dan was affected and asked, 'He was?'

'You completely broke Dan's heart!' Brad nodded his head with an intense stare right through me. Brad made me feel like I was completely clueless. 'You were all over him and then you dumped him for someone we all hate!'

'I never meant to hurt Dan and, for the record, I also liked Dom when I wasn't on E.'

This revelation forced Brad to take a different tact. 'When are you not on E? You don't even realise you're still in the honeymoon phase of that drug wearing off. And what about John? I suppose that is over now?'

⁓

John was delighted to see me again, and gave me a big hug when I joined him for his weekly gay radio broadcast. However, when I quickly pulled away from John's embrace, he knew something had changed. 'What's up?'

'I've met someone,' I smiled.

John smiled at my answer and didn't sound bothered at all, but rather interested. 'Who is he? Tell me all about him!'

I gave John a rundown on what had happened while I'd been in Sydney. John could tell that while I was happy to have met Dom, there was also

something bothering me. 'Is there a problem? You seem unhappy for someone who's just fallen in love.'

'How long does it take to get an AIDS test?'

'About four weeks. Don't tell me you let this guy—'

'Yes, I know it was fucking stupid, and now it's all I can think about. I'm
fully freaking out. Also, I'm coming down and feeling so depressed.'

The following day, John accompanied me to the local medical centre.
I felt so humiliated having to request a blood test for HIV. Embarrassed
and stupid, admitting I had unprotected sex, I worried that I'd caught the
virus. The needle hurt as it pierced the vein in the crease of my left arm to
draw enough blood to determine my fate. For the next two days, I sported a
bright pink Band-Aid stuck on the middle of my elbow that was surrounded
by a purple bruise. It was a constant reminder of what John told me was an
unbelievably poor decision considering HIV infections were still on the rise.

MAGIC MUSHROOMS

'NATHAN, I MISS you so much!' Dom told me through the phone line.

'Me too!' I felt a flood of relief. I was glad Dom phoned me. It showed he was thinking of me.

'I missed you so much I had to jerk off in the bathroom at work today!' Dom laughed. 'I kept getting hard-ons thinking about us having sex and had to, you know.'

'For real?' What Dom had said shocked me. I couldn't imagine someone doing such a thing, masturbating at work. 'You're kidding, right?'

'No, for real. I can't stop thinking about you, Nathan.'

'Me too, Dom,' I replied but didn't tell him the other reason he was on my mind, as I ran my fingers over the hot pink Band-Aid still covering the needle puncture wound from my first HIV test.

'I'm getting horny just hearing the sound of your voice,' Dom crooned.

The second I heard his deep voice utter those words, I felt my dick grow firm under my jeans. I waited a while before I admitted, 'So am I…'

'I've got my hand on my cock right now. It's pretty hard,' Dom's tone lowered to a primal groan.

I was glad I recently got a phone installed in my dorm room. Otherwise, I'd be very self-conscious to have this type of conversation in my dorm's living room. 'Wish I was there.' I took the bait.

'Really? What would you do to me?'

My answer led Dom to have a loud orgasm in my phone's earpiece.

Each long-distance phone conversation with Dom ended in ejaculation. This is how we kept our sexual connection alive whist being so far apart. Long-distance love phone sex. Dom called every night. I was amazed he didn't just forget about me the minute the drugs wore off, and I left Sydney, the way Brad had predicted. If anything, my connection with Dom was growing stronger with each heated phone call. I wondered if this was proof that I'd found real love. That Dom was being true to his words from the first morning we went to bed. He was sick of the gay scene, one-night stands, and wanted me to be his forever boyfriend.

In between the phone sex, I learnt more about Dom's background. When he had been at high school, he had been part of the rugby team because of his height and build. He'd been as big as now since Dom was sixteen years old. At school, he pretended to be straight. Then he claimed he had sex with some of the boys on his team, including the captain. Even though those boys were meant to be straight, they were up for taking one for the team from the alpha male, Dom, who'd played forward.

While I had always been terrible at sports, I never had such experiences. I was totally jealous of Dom's sordid high school history.

Dom also revealed he pretended to be straight, so much so that he got engaged to his high school sweetheart, Sonya, at age nineteen. But it all fell apart when she caught him in bed with the local North Shore male aerobics' instructor.

'The scandal outed me to the Beacon Hill community in a big way!' Dom chuckled. 'That's why I moved to Surry Hills. I was the talk of the town!'

'You were engaged to a girl?'

'For a whole year before it fell apart!'

After a few weeks of sexually charged phone conversations, I revealed to Dom that I was planning to go to a local Tropical Fruits dance party in the Northern Rivers region with Brad, Claire, and John.

'I don't want you to go without me!' Dom sounded uneasy and insecure.

'You don't have anything to worry about,' I assured him. 'I should be more worried about you being out on the gay scene in Sydney without me!'

'You can trust me,' Dom said earnestly. 'Promise.'

'Me too. It's magic mushroom season here. We're going 'shrooming, a natural high, that's all! I've never done mushrooms before. But you don't need to worry. I'll be there with Brad, Claire, and my ex, John. They'll look after me.'

'Brad? That totally hot guy who completely ignored me?' Dom sounded both annoyed and concerned. 'Who is this guy, John, your ex?'

The sketchy details I provided to Dom had the opposite effect.

'I'm going to join you!' Dom announced with a voice filled with determination.

Little did I realise the power of my words. They inspired Dom to get behind the wheel of his Toyota and speed up the Pacific Highway on a ten-hour drive to Lismore. I couldn't tell if this was because Dom didn't trust me or that he really loved me. Or was it that Dom was wise enough to know that when you're young, gay, and off your face with other handsome gay men, anything could happen and usually did. After all, that's how Dom had seduced me and stolen me from Dan.

The day before Dom arrived in Lismore, John took Brad, Claire, and I for a drive to the nearby farming town of Alstonville. We cruised past farm fields in search of magic mushrooms, a free, organic, natural, and potentially danger-ous even deadly high. None of us really thought anything bad could happen. We were at our bulletproof age, except for John. He should have known better. John was trying to be cool and was reliving his youth being a mature student.

John stopped his ute at a field which was deserted apart from several grazing cows. We carefully climbed a rusted barbed-wire fence. 'This is per-fect!' John announced as we each carefully stepped on the long yellow-green grass and tried to avoid putting our shoes into a large, dried dropping of cow dung. The cow droppings had baked into large round disks from the blazing sun.

'So how will we know if we've found the right kind of mushroom?' asked Claire.

'You'll know. They have gold tops, and they grow out of the dung,' John advised and laughed intensely.

'Gross!' Claire's face screwed up and she waved her hands to get rid of the reality of what we were doing.

'This makes scoring drugs in the city seem rather civilised compared to getting an organic high in the country!' Brad quipped.

'Don't be such princesses.' John still laughed intensely. 'We'll wash them and dip them in honey before eating them.'

'Found one!' Claire pointed to a small mushroom that sat on top of a pile of dried cow dung. We each rushed to see what she'd found. It was a tiny white mushroom with a perfect gold shine on the top that was around seven centimeters in diameter.

'Yep, we've struck gold!' John smiled enthusiastically. That one mushroom led to the us to playing a fun game of connect the golden dots scattered through the farm paddock. Plucking magic mushrooms from shit. By the end of our hunt, we'd filled a small plastic bag full of what we hoped were magic mushrooms.

~

Dom arrived the following Saturday morning. He parked his dust-covered Toyota in the university dorm parking lot. I was overjoyed seeing him in my doorway. It didn't matter that Dom's eyes were bloodshot and his face was oily from staying up all night being on the road. I threw my arms around him and kissed him passionately. I didn't care who saw us. 'Can't believe you did this!' I released Dom from my arms.

'That was one fucking long drive!' Dom exclaimed. 'This party better be worth it.'

'Just wait, it will be!' I assured Dom leading him to my dorm room.

Even though Dom had been up all night, the first thing he did when we entered my room was slam the door shut and push me onto the squeaky single mattress. Dom jumped on my body and pulled off my clothes. As we kissed, we didn't care if my two roommates could hear every noise through the thin brick walls.

~

The Tropical Fruits dance party was held in a small church hall near the country town of Channon. In the darkness, Dom followed a convoy of red tail-lights, navigating the winding and barely paved road through the hills. My hand was busy squeezing Dom's muscular leg for most of the journey.

One of the vehicles we followed was John's ute. John had Brad and Claire as passengers. Eventually, the cars stopped outside a small weatherboard wooden church on a mountain surrounded by tall trees. The windows of the church hall were flashing with multi-coloured lights and the electronic beats of the song '*Such a good feeling*', by Brothers in Rhythm was playing loud enough to be heard from the outside.

In the parking lot, I introduced Dom to John and Claire.

'My, you're a big boy!' John did his usual intense awkward laugh.

'John!' Claire smirked. 'You're embarrassing him.'

'I'm six-foot-five.' Dom chuckled. 'I've heard it all before.'

'Dom, you remember Brad,' I smiled.

'Hi, Dom.' Brad looked away, displeased to see Dom again in person.

'Brad, be nice!' I spoke up, annoyed.

'I think that'll take more than a few magic mushrooms!' Brad responded sarcastically and still avoiding eye contact.

'What a good idea.' John tried to smooth over the uncomfortable atmosphere between Brad and Dom. John opened the glove box and retrieved a bag full of honey covered magic mushrooms. He handed us each a spoon as he passed the plastic bag around. We each scooped out a few slimy, shiny, honey coated mushroom and put them in our mouths. The sweet locally produced organic honey covered the vile taste of the gold tops.

'It's best not to chew them,' John warned a bit too late for me.

After we had swallowed a couple of handfuls of mushrooms, we were ready to join the locals entering the hall. Inside the hall was a large space with wooden floorboards about to be used as a dancefloor. At the end of the hall was a stage where a local DJ played Right Said Fred's, 'I'm too sexy'.

We each bopped our heads to the beat and mouthed the words to the novelty song. Flashing coloured lights illuminated the room as the gathering gays and lesbians moved to the music.

It was so different to a city nightclub situation. There was plenty of space to dance. Yet this didn't stop the room from getting hot and sweaty within a few hours. A gathering of just over one-hundred people became good friends, enjoying having a boogie in the middle of the country. Especially when they witnessed Dom dancing like he was on top of one of the podiums of DCM. As usual, my new boyfriend became the centre of attention.

'Did he eat a particularly potent mushroom?' John laughed with a slight bitchy tone to Brad and Claire, who both burst into laughter at his observation. High on magic mushrooms, Brad and Claire laughed just as intensely as John did. I got annoyed overhearing them and when they continued to laugh hysterically, high on magic mushrooms.

'Shut up!' I laughed as there was a small part of me that also found the observation funny. However, what I overheard also made me sad.

'I can't believe Nathan would be attracted to someone as pretentious as that!' Claire yelled in Brad's ear, just loud enough for me to overhear.

Brad responded intentionally loud enough so I would hear. 'None of us can. It's like Nathan can't see what we see!'

I ignored them and went to dance with my boyfriend.

Dom was dancing in his own happy magic mushroom world, blissfully unaware of the insults aimed at him. Dom's over-energetic dancing ensured he became the free entertainment for the night. The mixed crowd of young and mature queer people couldn't believe what they were seeing as Dom did his best dance moves to ward off my ex-boyfriend John and to impress Brad. Only Dom's efforts resulted in the opposite effect.

I didn't have the heart to tell Dom the truth. I thought Dom was fun to be with, a superstar from DCM. To Brad and Claire, Dom was an overbearing, annoying, and pretentious attention seeker.

I focused on the happy expressions on the faces of the gay men and women of the Northern Rivers inside the church hall. At least, they seemed to be enjoying the free dance routine that was my boyfriend, dancing Dom on magic mushrooms.

Completely out-of-it and unaware of how other people were reacting to him, Dom yelled in my ear, 'This crowd is so old it's making me feel so young!'

I laughed as I felt like there was more than just lights flashing around me when the psilocybin I'd digested took a firm hold over my senses. I felt like I was floating across the dance floor rather than dancing. There were also visual sparkles twinkling wherever I looked.

Just before dawn, a sweat soaked Dom said he needed some air. He took my hand and lead me outside. Together, we wandered under the moonlit night sky, up the hill towards the privacy of the trees. Alone and far enough away from the church hall, Dom and I pulled down each other's jeans. I sucked Dom's large dick in the darkness and couldn't believe it when Dom let his load go in my mouth without warning. It was the first time I had ever tasted cum.

'Let me suck you!' Dom breathed heavily. I stood up obediently as Dom got down on his knees and swallowed my cock. He moved his lips along the shaft until his chin rested against my balls. The feeling was so intense my legs trembled. 'Come in my mouth,' Dom instructed and within seconds I obliged. The orgasm was intensified from being so high.

After, we embraced and kissed each other. Even though I was high, I couldn't believe what I'd just done. I couldn't believe how far I was willing to go with Dom. I suspected what we'd done meant I'd have to get re-tested for HIV.

Four weeks later, I got the results of my blood tests.

'You're HIV negative,' the middle-aged doctor told me with zero expression. At first, I panicked, thinking the term negative meant something was seriously wrong, that I had AIDS. Upon seeing the concern spread across my face, the doctor leaned forward. 'Negative means you're okay. You don't have HIV. Please be more careful next time, Nathan. Always use a condom. Always!'

SHOPPING SPREE

'NATHAN, I LOVE you dearly, but there's no way I can do that frigging drive to see you in Lismore ever again.' Dom told me after he transferred two hundred dollars into my bank account. I used the money to buy a return train ticket to visit him in Sydney.

'Then I'm happy to come to you. Even if it means missing classes.'

All I cared about was the fun I would have with Dom. Fortunately, there were no assignments due during the week, so I figured I could get away with playing hooky just this once. Besides, I was studying easy subjects like marketing and public relations, so I didn't think getting away would do any harm.

Nothing mattered except for the opportunity to be with Dom. Being in love with Dom was a stronger addiction than the most mind-bending drug I had ever tried. It was all consuming. It felt so good. I was complete. But as with all drugs, the withdrawal was hard to cope with. Being away from the source of my newfound psychological high caused me to crash and make increasingly poor decisions.

My heart melted the instant I saw Dom waiting for me at the Central Station train platform when the Country Link XPT train pulled into the Sydney platform, just before midday.

'I got you a surprise!' Dom said as he took me in his arms and hugged me tight. He didn't give a damn who saw us embrace in broad day light. Dom handed me a tiny navy-blue box. Curious, I opened it to find a shiny white gold, triple-banded Russian wedding ring. 'I want everyone to know you're mine! Does it fit?'

As I put the ring on, I wondered how much it cost. It looked very expensive. 'Yeah, it's a good fit!' I announced with pride as I admired my new jewellery on my left hand. 'Does this mean we're engaged?'

'It does! I only want to be with you, Nathan.'

'Me too, Dom,' I was so touched. This was the first piece of jewellery I'd ever worn. It felt good. We were a real couple. Young love. Just me and Dom.

'I have another surprise for you, darling!' Dom grabbed my overnight backpack with one hand and my hand with his other. We walked along the platform happily holding hands. 'We're going to meet Tiffany. She's got a—' Dom paused, like he forgot what he was about to say. 'She's got an advance on her recording contract.'

I thought it was strange the way Dom hesitated as he said this. 'An advance? When does her music come out?' I asked excited.

'Any day now,' Dom responded vaguely.

'Oh my god that is so exciting!' While I had enjoyed listening to the tape Tiffany had given me of her dance music, I didn't think it sounded ready to be played in the clubs. She must have worked very hard with her band, Elemental, to get it ready for release, I pondered.

Driving from Central Station into the city, Dom parked in the Queen Victoria Building car park. We met Tiffany later. She was waiting outside Grace Brothers in Pitt Street Mall. She was holding a stack of shopping bags, each with a logo from the most expensive designer stores in town from Calvin Klein, Morrissey Edmiston, and Versace. Upon seeing me, Tiffany dropped her bags by her sides and opened her arms to give me a big squeeze. 'Hello, sweetheart!'

'Dom tells me you got an advance!' I was happy for Tiffany's success. 'When are they going to release your music?'

'Soon!' Tiffany winked and turned to Dom. 'Where are you parked? I need to drop these off!'

'You must have got a big advance by the looks of things,' I said with my eyes on the shopping bags.

'Oh, that's just the start, honey.' Tiffany grinned. 'I've got a nice new shiny credit card to play with today.'

'Tiffany is taking us on a shopping spree to spend her advance!' Dom announced.

I was taken aback. I hadn't planned on an afternoon of shopping. Having slept poorly on the over-night train, I was feeling weary and just wanted to head back to Dom's bedroom. While I loved to go shopping as much as any gay man, it was no substitute for sex.

After dropping the shopping bags into the boot of Dom's car, I got into the swing of the shopping spree when Tiffany bought me a leather jacket at David Jones.

'But it's so expensive!' It didn't feel right. I began to pull the jacket off.

Dom hung it back on my shoulders like he was dressing a Ken doll. 'But it suits you so much, baby!' Dom tried to convince me.

I looked at my reflection in the mirror. I loved the way the black leather biker jacket looked on me. It was so Marlon Brando. I looked just as hot as he had in 'The Wild Ones'.

'Nathan, you look so hot! We must buy that for you!' Tiffany agreed with Dom.

'Fuck, how much was your advance, Tiffany?' I exclaimed.

'Secret!' Tiffany responded.

For the rest of the day, Tiffany was charging everything to her shiny platinum credit card. 'I'm loaded now that I'm officially an up-and-coming underground pop star!' Tiffany bragged. She spent so much money even though her record company hadn't even released her music. I thought it normally happened the other way around. First your music gets released, and then if you're super-lucky it becomes a hit in the clubs or on radio and then you get paid royalties. Wasn't that when the cash came rolling in? Central Station Records must really believe in Elemental! They paid Tiffany an advance! Or so I thought.

'This would look so good on you, Nathan!' Dom was holding up a USA gridiron style mesh top that had a 1970s look about it.

'Wow!' I was sleep deprived and easily distracted.

'Charge it!' Tiffany announced flamboyantly to the sales assistant who was busy folding clothes into tissue paper and packing them into shopping bags.

Next, we drove to the boutique stores on Crown Street. It felt so glamorous strolling along the sidewalk with Dom and Tiffany as we each held fancy shopping bags.

'Now I know how it must feel to be a wealthy trust-fund kid!' I joked. Today was a contrast to the reality of being a financially struggling student who was being supported by his parents. Now I was being spoiled by my new boyfriend and ex-girlfriend. Funny how life turns out.

'Isn't this, like, the most fun ever!' Tiffany exclaimed as I felt like people on the street were literally starring at us like we were celebrities as we passed the vintage store 'Route 66'. The shopping spree high was like an illicit high. However, the excitement got too much for Tiffany towards the end of the day when we hit the last store on the list, 'Wheels & Doll Baby'.

I was checking out a series of ironic and provocative T-shirts on a rack by the shop window. The T-shirts had screen prints of ironic logos such as, 'The Betty Ford Centre', and 'The Sex-Kittens' in the style of 'The Sex Pistols'. I was vaguely aware of Tiffany as she approached Dom. Trying to be as discrete as she possibly could, Tiffany whispered something into Dom's ear.

'What do you mean?' I heard Dom laugh. I popped over to find out what was up.

'What's my name on the card?' Tiffany hissed to Dom as she tried not to appear suspicious in front of the sales assistant. The assistant was tapping the shiny platinum credit card impatiently, waiting for Tiffany to sign the receipt. What I heard Dom say in response to Tiffany's question made a shiver go up my spine.

'Sheba Krishnan!' Dom said in a low voice.

I watched as Tiffany returned to the cash register to sign the receipt, I quickly asked Dom, 'Who's Sheba?'

'No one,' Dom answered quickly. 'How are you going, babe?'

'So tired!' I answered. However, I wanted to get the bottom of what just happened. 'Did Tiffany run out of credit or something?'

'No, she, um, she wasn't sure if that top suited her or not,' Dom replied with a straight face.

'Looked good to me,' I said as I pretended not be aware of what just had happened.

Even with sleep deprivation, it dawned on me that as we had bounced from shop to shop all afternoon, spending thousands of dollars, clearly it was not on Tiffany's card. Rather, someone named Sheba was paying. Who on Earth would think that a white girl's name would be Sheba? I wondered who Sheba was and if she knew she was carrying the cost of Tiffany's purchases. My heart sank as I pretended not to suspect something was wrong. I started to wonder if I should confront Dom and Tiffany, or keep my mouth shut.

~

'Which one are you going to wear?' Dom asked as we admired the spoils of an afternoon's worth of non-stop shopping displayed across his queen size doona cover. Designer shopping bags were sprawled recklessly across the floor. I still hadn't said anything about what I suspected about the credit card.

'I still can't believe you guys bought all this stuff!' I felt numb, knowing that the designer clothes we were about to wear, were likely ill-gotten. I was growing concerned that something didn't add up. I pretended to be cool with what was going on, not wanting to appear like I was a square. I wondered if this was the first time Tiffany and Dom had done such a thing. They always wore the coolest and most expensive clothes. For the first time, I wondered how they managed to do so. I think this weekend I just found out. This is how dedicated they were as club kids; they went to extreme lengths to ensure they wore the latest brands and fashion trends.

'I wanted today to be a big surprise! That's why I sent you money so you could join us!' Dom smiled. 'I want my man to get what he wants!'

'Yeah? Well, I've already got that, Dom. I got you. That's all I want!' I smiled and flashed the stylish ring on my finger. Then, immediately I wondered if the ring was paid for by that shiny credit card. While I loved material possessions just as much as the next Generation-X club kid, I knew the stack of designer shopping bags discarded on the floor were no substitute for having someone to love. Material possessions certainly weren't worth getting into trouble over.

That night, after making the difficult decision of what illegally purchased outfit to wear from the high-priced collection, I did my best to ignore the troubling feeling that was taking hold. Instead, I tried my best to embrace the pleasure of looking glamorous in a pair of brand-new Calvin Klein jeans and US 70s-inspired Grid Iron mesh football jersey that was numbered 69. The top showed off my thin muscular chest and abs to great effect — very sexy. Getting dressed in new designer labels made me feel like a male model, especially after blurring reality with a few lines of crystal white powder.

When I stepped out of the apartment with Tiffany, Dom, and Mark, I felt totally cool. We were dedicated club kids who strutted our stuff down Oxford Street on a pilgrimage to DCM while sporting the latest fashion. No more did I wear second hand retro vintage clothes from op shops like Vinnies. However, if I'd known what Dom and Tiffany's shopping spree would cost us all in the long run, I would have chosen to stay single, miserable, and lonely in a country town university.

Saturday night was a blur of familiar beautiful faces and adoring strangers admiring our cutting-edge clothes. The feeling of being the centre of attention was heightened with each line of cocaine we snorted from Mark's stash in the nightclub's toilet cubicles, a special place. It was where Dom and I'd first kissed. How sweet it was returning to the scene of the crime where we became boyfriends.

On the steamy dance floor, we were approached by a photographer to have our picture taken. The photographer said the picture was for the free street press clubbers' bible, '3-D Magazine'.

'Strike a pose!' Dom grinned as he stretched his arms around the people he loved most in the world. Our infamy had just begun with the blinding flash of a paparazzi camera. I couldn't believe how much fun it was to feel this way, being on a chemical high, wearing the latest fashion, and suddenly not having a care in the world or connection with reality as night slipped into day. The feelings of concern I'd experienced earlier in the evening vanished overnight and transformed into chemically induced confidence, a sense of invincibility after countless lines. Although, that confidence did take a hit when I spotted Brad's friends, Stevie and Emma, on the dance floor. I decided to approach them, feeling like a million bucks.

'Hi guys!'

'Did you hear something?' Stevie shouted to Emma so I would hear as he pretended not to see me.

Emma looked around and gave me a dirty, disapproving look. 'No, but something smells!'

As Stevie and Emma continued to dance, I realised Brad's friends held a serious grudge against me for the way I hooked up with Dom over Dan.

I returned to my boyfriend, ex-girlfriend, and her drug-dealing boyfriend, Mark, for comfort.

After dancing all night like we owned DCM and later The Taxi Club till day light, we returned to Dom's apartment to spend Sunday morning bragging to a bunch of new hangers-on.

'Keep an eye out for us in 3-D magazine!' Dom informed Mark's new followers with pride. I didn't know or care about a single first name. They were all loyal clients of Mark. And little did Dom realise, but soon his name would make it into a mainstream newspaper for all the wrong reasons.

By Sunday afternoon, Dom and I were alone in his bedroom. I watched with excitement the sight of our naked reflection on the queen-sized bed in the wardrobe mirrors. In my mind, it was a vision of perfection, something I'd always dreamed would come true. The moment I was alone with Dom, having just popped a free ecstasy pill from Mark, I didn't know where I began and Dom ended. It was the first time I was able to take Dom. Neither of us felt a condom was needed. We both believed each other when confessing that neither of us had HIV. With all our senses switched on, I was so excited and turned on by Dom's body inside mine, I didn't need to touch myself to ejaculate. The orgasm following more than three hours of constant chemical fuelled sex was the most intense sensation I had ever experienced in my life. Through Dom, I discovered the male G-spot was a very real thing.

~

'Darn!' Dom cursed when we woke on Monday morning.

'What is it?' I asked groggy and barely awake.

'They want me to do a shift in Double Bay to cover someone who's sick,' Dom said putting on his uniform.

'You look so responsible!' I was impressed by how professional Dom looked. It was quite a transformation compared to the black leather pants, mesh-top, and a beaded crucifix necklace Dom had worn on Saturday night.

'Want to give me a lift to work?' Dom asked. 'You can have my car for the rest of the day to hang out if you like.'

I eagerly obliged and drove my man to the Double Bay branch. However, as I did my best to navigate the morning peak hour traffic, I wondered if it was safe for me to be driving. I was still feeling the chemical after effects from the weekend.

'I don't know how you can face work after all the drugs we took over the weekend!' I commented as I tried to focus on the road ahead. 'I'm coming down so bad right now!'

'You'll survive.' Dom smiled. 'I feel like shit, but work's work. It's where I go to rest,' Dom joked and kissed me on the lips before he got out. 'See you tonight, baby.'

To cut through the traffic, I took a detour through Paddington on my way back to Dom's apartment. As I did so, I absent-mindedly listened to Bass-o-Matic's 'Fascinating Rhythm' and sang along as I accidently took another detour, a wrong turn in front of an on-coming van. The collision activated the seatbelt's safety restraint as Dom's Toyota was flung backwards by the impact.

I had no idea what had just happened as the car suddenly faced the opposite direction to which I'd originally been driving. Everything stopped. Winded, dazed, and confused, I faced a smashed windscreen. In the process, my head had hit the steering wheel, and the oxygen was thrown out of my lungs. The seatbelt had held me in a vice like grip. It had saved my life, but at the same time it made me lose my breath.

'Call an ambulance!' I rasped to an onlooker who rushed to check if I was, okay.

The rest of the morning's events were a blur. The owner of the totalled van, an aggressive tradie, started abusing me, 'You don't fuckin' turn in front of an on-coming van, dickhead!'

There was a distant sound of an ambulance siren, growing louder. A tow truck turned up at the same time as the police did. Two constables took down details at the scene in a little black book. Once the paramedics arrived, they made an assessment that I was all right and didn't have concussion. After, they let me go as a tow truck driver hoisted Dom's mangled car onto a giant metal hook.

There was a diagonal black mark across my white Versace t-shirt from where the seat belt had protected me. In a drug-induced-come-down combined with the daze of surviving a head-on car collision, I wandered through the streets of Paddington and Surry Hills feeling lost and in shock.

That sensation changed to anxiety as I approached Dom's apartment building. I became concerned at the prospect of having to break the news of what I'd just done. I was not sure how to tell Dom I'd totalled his car. I was wearing a marked Versace t-shirt, with Calvin Klein jeans and Adidas sneakers. Each item was brought from the weekend's shopping spree. It was like I'd met with the police sporting evidence from Dom and Tiffany's credit crime spree.

The real hangover from the weekend had begun.

Nearly being killed was just the start of my problems.

TRASH BAGS

'WHAT HAPPENED?' TIFFANY'S jaw dropped upon seeing me enter the apartment with a bump on my forehead and black mark across my new designer brand T-shirt.

'I just totalled Dom's car,' I announced vacantly.

'Oh my God! Are you okay?'

I just burst into tears.

Tiffany hugged me. 'Oh, love, it's okay.' Tiffany said under her breath. 'Dom loves you more than his car.'

I spent the rest of the day staring at drab daytime TV, fascinated by the bad acting on, 'The Young and the Restless'. I was not really taking any of it in, just viewing it as a distraction counting the hours until Dom came home. To my surprise, when I revealed the news to Dom over the phone at lunch, to let him know the reason why I would not be picking him up from work, his reaction was not what I anticipated.

'You wrecked my car?' Dom asked. His voice went higher at the end of the question.

'I'm sorry.' I felt too exhausted to say any more. I was also still in a state of shock as the realisation grew that I could have killed myself driving when I knew I shouldn't have been. I was doing all the wrong things since meeting Dom.

'Thank God you're okay!' Dom exhaled. 'I don't know what I'd do without you. I couldn't live without you. Nathan, you're so cute, you're my baby, you belong to me.'

Unfortunately, it turned out Dom's car was uninsured and a write-off. Not only that, but Dom was up for $30,000 for the damages that I'd had caused to the tradesman's van and Dom's car. Apart from selling the brand-new clothes to make some fast cash, Dom was flat broke. He had no savings. He was a club kid, living beyond his means and only had credit card debt.

Unlike me, it wasn't like Dom could ask his parents for help. Dom's mum had barely spoken to him since she'd thought he'd embarrassed the family by getting with the male aerobics instructor and coming out a few weeks before he was supposed to get married. Their relationship was frosty at best. Even if she did have the money to bail her son out, Dom said he doubted she'd help.

As for Dom's father, Dom said his dad had passed away when Dom was a young boy. 'I'm fucked!' Dom placed his head in both hands as he sat on the bed and let out a deep breath.

'Could you take out a loan?' I suggested, trying to be helpful. 'Wouldn't you get a staff discount?'

~⁀

'What on Earth are you doing here?' My mum was startled to see me at her front door. 'You're meant to be at university!'

'I know,' I answered sheepishly as mum opened the security gate to let me in. 'I was in a car accident.'

'What? Are you okay?'

'I'm fine, but the car isn't. Neither is the one that hit me.'

'What on Earth are you doing in Sydney getting into car accidents? You're meant to be at university!' Mum's voice raised an octave. I felt that I had no choice but to beg my parents for help to bail out my new boyfriend, someone who they'd never even met. I felt responsible for what had happened. I hoped my parents would offer to foot the bill for the car-wreck that was the result of my first serious relationship.

'You bloody idiot!' Dad fumed after I explained what happened. 'What the hell are you doing skipping university? We're paying a fortune for you to study in Lismore!'

'I know; it was idiotic!' I conceded. 'I'll never do it again.'

'Are you on drugs again, Nathan?' Dad's face was filled with frustration.

'Of course not!' I lied, even though I was still coming down from excessive drug taking on the weekend.

'Skipping university! Asking us for money for someone we've never met. You've got to be kidding, Nathan.' My mother shook her head disapprovingly. 'Is this how you think your father deserves to celebrate his sixtieth birthday?'

'His what?' My heart sank as I realised, I'd forgotten all about my dad's sixtieth birthday.

'What a bloody brilliant birthday present this is!' Dad scoffed and left the hallway in disgust and retreated upstairs. 'You've really done it this time, Nathan!'

I feared this meant I'd pushed my luck too far and broken the unspoken trust and faith my parents had in me. I'd completely lost control of my life and what I was getting mixed up in.

'And what's that ring on your finger all about?' Mum asked angrily, spotting the shiny metal around my ring finger.

~

The following day, for some reason, Dad handed over a bank cheque for $30,000. When he gave me the cheque, he let me know that this was money he and mum had been saving for me since I was a baby. They intended to give me this money when I turned twenty-one. The intention was for the money to go towards my first home deposit — to set me up financially — not cover the costs of being a reckless teenager. And never in their worst nightmares would my parents ever have guessed what they were really saving up for was their son's reckless boyfriend.

Dom couldn't believe I was able to bail him out.

'Nathan, you're the most special guy in the world,' his voice quivered. 'I don't know what to say. Most people would have just washed their hands of the whole thing. But not you.'

'I'm not most people,' I replied, realising my relationship with Dom was costing me so much, not just friends, but now tens of thousands of dollars. 'I'm still in disbelief my parents helped.'

'They must seriously love you and want to keep you out of trouble!'

'I guess so,' I said as it started to dawn on me how much this relationship changing my life. And not for the better.

A week later, when I was back in Lismore, Dom phoned me as usual.

'Something unexpected happened at work today,' he began casually. 'I thought nothing of it when a well-dressed Indian lady came to collect her credit card. My heart froze the second she presented her driver's license, and I read the name — Sheba Krishnan.' Dom didn't need to say anything more. I now knew it was the name Tiffany had been signing all over town on that stupid Saturday with her shiny platinum credit card. 'I don't know why, but I never expected to come face to face with the card's actual owner. Not in my wildest dreams!' Dom laughed nervously.

'What did you do?' I asked fearing what Dom and Tiffany had done was going to get us all in trouble.

'I nearly had a heart attack! I didn't know what I was going to do, considering I'd already handed over Sheba's card to Tiffany. I went through the motions, acting like nothing was wrong so it wouldn't look suspicious. I got the key for the security box where all the credit cards are stored, knowing all along that Sheba's wouldn't be there when I opened it. I had no choice but to follow company procedure and report the card missing.'

'Shit.'

'This means I am the one who triggered an internal investigation into the unauthorised release of the card that I handed over to Tiffany.'

'Oh my God! You're going to go to jail!'

'You don't know that, Nathan. They have to prove it first.'

'How could you and Tiffany be so stupid? I can't believe you got me involved in this!'

The next day, just before class, Brad took me aside. 'Listen, you didn't hear it from me, but you need to drop Dom, like yesterday!'

'Why?' I was tired of Brad constantly picking on my boyfriend, even though I had begun to have similar thoughts myself.

'He's bad news!' Brad exclaimed. 'Apparently, Dom, and your best friend Tiffany, dropped off a bunch of trash bags filled with something dodgy to Ricky and Aaron's place.'

'They what?' My heart sank. I could guess the trash bags were filled with essential clubbing gear: Calvin Klein, Morrissey Edmiston, Versace, and Wheels & Doll Baby.

'For real!' Brad waved his hand between us dramatically. 'They're fully freaking out because they think the police are onto them.'

I felt flushed the instant Brad uttered these words. That feeling of having the wind taken out of me, which I recently experienced following the car crash, returned.

'Best you know now before you get in too deep. I think things are about to turn ugly,' Brad warned ominously.

That night, the usual long-distance phone sex I looked forward to with Dom was replaced by an awkward conversation to seek the truth. 'Dom, is there something you want to tell me?'

'About what?' Dom asked completely aloof. Like everything was fine.

'Brad told me about your visit to Ricky and Aaron's.' I didn't want to say what I knew over the phone, fearing the police could be taping Dom's phone line.

There was just silence on the other end of the line. 'What does Brad know?' Dom finally asked.

'He knows. You're going to get caught!' I said, unable to hide my frustration.

'I didn't tell you because I wanted to protect you. The less you know about what's going down, the better. It's not like we've been caught. It's just a precaution; it was still worth it.'

'Are you fucking kidding? How could you be so stupid?' I was exasperated. 'I love you, Dom, but what you guys did changes everything.'

'What do you mean it changes everything? Nathan, I love you!'

'I love you too, but I can't believe you got me involved in something so fucking stupid!'

'Is everything okay?' I heard Tiffany ask Dom in the background.

'Ricky blabbed!' Dom told Tiffany.

'Shit!' Tiffany cursed. 'What an asshole. Mark! You've got to tell Aaron to get Ricky to shut his mouth! Or we'll all be in deep shit.'

'Nathan, everything will be fine,' Dom tried to reassure me in an oddly calm tone. 'Just stay cool until this blows over. Everything will be all right. You'll see.'

Even though I had intended to end my relationship with Dom over the phone, words failed me. I just couldn't do it. Apart from the crime thing, Dom was the most perfect man I'd ever met. Or so I'd thought. Now it was all fucked up. I loved him deeply, though that love was now mixed with regret and fear of what the future held.

After hanging up the phone, I looked at the three gold bands that were intertwined around each other on my ring finger. As I studied the Russian wedding ring Dom had given me, I now knew for sure he hadn't bought it with his hard-earned money, but rather purchased it with a stolen credit card. Suddenly, it wasn't a symbol of Dom's love and commitment to me. The shiny ring was nothing more than a symbol of three people — Dom, Tiffany, and I — intertwined in a criminal affair.

The following day, I had to talk to someone. I knew I couldn't confide in Brad. He would only tell me to stop being an idiot and dump Dom as soon as possible. So would John or Claire, if I chose to confide in them. I was smart enough to know I had to avoid spreading my knowledge about the crime any further. This is what prompted me to book an appointment with one of the university's counsellors that Claire had seen. Because as their brochure said, 'Students can talk confidentially and freely to one of our accredited counsellors anytime about anything.'

The next afternoon, I found myself sitting facing a total stranger and, to my own surprise, I blurted out what was going on in my life, trauma dumped, confessing what was *troubling* me.

The trained counsellor found it hard to contain his surprise, especially upon learning that I had no intention of splitting up with my boyfriend who was exhibiting incredibly poor judgement and dragging me down with him.

'And you're still with this guy?' the counsellor's voice raised an octave.

'I love him!' I answered with sincerity.

'But you've only known him for how many months?' The counsellor tilted his head.

'A few months.' I looked away. Hearing myself, it did sound ridiculous. Yet I'd convinced myself I was in love. I'd had the most intense sexual experiences of my life with Dom.

'Dump him!' the therapist advised. The session provided no comfort at all. It only reinforced what I'd already come to realise, that I'd made a massive mistake for hooking up with Dom over Dan. The therapist was on Brad's side. Brad's words echoed in my mind, *You need to drop Dom*.

A POLICE FORCE MATTER

27 NOVEMBER 1991

THE CASSETTE TAPE continued to play Dom's police interview, and I regretted several life decisions.

'Mr James, you already told us you can't remember how many times the card was used. Can you tell me in which stores the card was used?'

'Um, I remember it being used at Grace Brothers, but as you said, not at which counter, or what was purchased, and honestly that's about it. There's nothing more I can tell you.'

'Would you care to tell us, and bear in mind we understand your limited memory of this day, your version of the events that day? Say, from the time you went out with Tiffany and…?'

'Nathan. I don't remember the day totally clearly, but for much of the morning, Nathan was not with us. He was coming down from Lismore by train, and I picked him up at about 12 o'clock. Um, we had been out shopping with the card prior to that. I can't remember what shops we'd been too before collecting Nathan.'

'Can you estimate how many stores you and Tiffany went to and purchase goods with this card?'

'No, I cannot.'

'Not even say, a number between 1 and 20?'

'No. I can only remember 2 stores.'

'Mr James, I put it to you that you're lying about your knowledge of the events on 14 September.' The Detective paused. 'The time is 6:30pm I'm just going to suspend this interview to confer with my colleague.'

⁓

'The time is approximately 6:45pm this interview now resumes. Thank you. Sorry about the short break. I'm going to show you a voucher for the value of $194, dated 14 September, at 12:36pm. What can you tell me about that voucher?'

'I can't say anything. Nothing comes to mind about that voucher.'

'Can you tell me about the signature that appears at the bottom of that voucher?'

'It's signed, Sheba Krishnan.'

'Can you tell me who signed that?'

'Once again, it was Tiffany, so I assume it was her.'

'Can you tell me, bearing in mind we understand you have limited memory in relation to this particular day, when all these vouchers and transactions took place? Can you remember leaving Tiffany at any time on that day while you were shopping?'

'Yes, I can. When I went to pick up Nathan, and when Nathan was getting changed, and getting some food, et cetera.'

'Can you tell me how many hours you were shopping for?'

'No, I can't.'

'Can you remember what you did with the merchandise that you purchased, whether you left it at the store, or what you did with it?'

'It was all brought home. I did not carry anything, and after that it was there for anyone in the unit to make use of. There were always people staying in the unit at any given time. But after it was discovered by the bank, I washed my hands clean of it. I told Tiffany I didn't want to have anything more to do with it. I don't know what happened to it. It was all given back to Tiffany, and I said I wanted nothing more to do with it.'

'Did you, Tiffany, or Nathan carry all the merchandise back to your residence?'

'Tiffany carried most of it. And as I said, Nathan didn't know the card was not Tiffany's, and he didn't see any vouchers being signed and didn't know nothing about the name on the card.'

'And you didn't carry anything?'

'No.'

'Can you tell me why you didn't carry anything? Bearing in mind, there's a fair amount of goods there?'

Dom laughed at this suggestion, nervously.

'I don't carry anything, I'm not Tiffany's carting horse. I drove that day, and I didn't drive home as I had a bad headache.'

'But can you tell me, bearing in mind Tiffany and your friend carried the goods, where were the goods placed?'

'I assume in the boot of my car.'

'Can you remember them being put in the boot of your car?'

'Somebody put them in the boot.'

'And what happened when you got home?'

'I honestly don't remember'

'Again, I put it to you that you're lying to us about your knowledge of these events.'

'Honestly, I'm not lying, I just don't remember.'

'What type of car do you drive or were the goods put into?'

'At that time, I had a Toyota.'

'So, the car was pretty well stacked up?'

'Once again, I wouldn't have a clue.'

'Can you name any of the merchandise purchased on that day?'

'I remember one pair of pants, ah — pair of flared pants — I'm struggling to remember it at all.'

'Apart from the clothes, is there anything else you can remember?'

'No.'

'I'm now going to show you another voucher, but I must remind you again that you're not obliged to say anything, but anything you do say can be used as evidence against you. Do you understand that?'

'Yes, I do.'

'I'm now going to show you voucher to the value of $209. What do you know of this?'

'It's signed by Sheba Krishnan, that's all I know.'

'Can you give me an estimate, based on your limited memory, as to the total value of the goods that were purchased on this day?'

'I've been told by the bank it was in the vicinity of $4,000, which I've repaid or made restitution to that from my superannuation and severance payment.'

'And you agree that you did make some restitution to the bank. Can you tell me why you made restitution to the bank?'

'Because I felt that I was responsible for giving the card to Tiffany, and I didn't want it to cause any aggravation between myself and the bank and the law. I thought I was doing the right thing by trying not to provoke the law or anyone else further. I was trying to clear the matter up.'

'Did Tiffany make any restitution to the bank?'

'No, she did not.'

'Do you know where Tiffany is now?'

'No. I do not. I have a number for Tiffany's mum, but each time I've called it, I've been told she's not there.'

COMPENSATION

D OM'S CRIMINAL ACTIVITY did nothing for our long-distance phone sex. There were more sordid details for Dom to discuss. It wasn't just our lives that changed for the worse from Dom and Tiffany's misguided decision to go on a shopping spree with a fraudulent credit card. It also affected many of the good club kids on the Oxford Street scene, the ones who relied on Mark's services. The police investigation included a search warrant of Dom, Mark, and Tiffany's apartment.

Mark was busted.

It was under Mark and Tiffany's bed that the detectives discovered evidence more incriminating than designer labels. They found designer drugs: fifty ecstasy pills, one-hundred satchels of speed, and over $10,000 in cash. Dom denied all knowledge of what was in Mark and Tiffany's bedroom.

Mark's operation was abruptly shut down. Dom said there were rumours spread around DCM and the Midnight Shift about what had happened to the guy who dealt from the back booth.

'Seriously, the phone hasn't stop ringing with people asking where else they could score.' Dom sounded annoyed. 'It's not like I'm not in enough trouble already without adding being accessory to drug dealing!'

I could tell Dom wasn't taking this seriously. If anything, he thought the situation was funny because he laughed while I grew increasingly uncomfortable.

For a while everything had seemed so wonderful with Dom. I'd felt so grown-up when I'd lived momentarily at Dom's. The realisation that my boyfriend was living beyond the law should have been a red flag. I couldn't believe how naive I'd been about everything. I felt like I was a stupid, inexperienced club kid without a clue.

'Mark and Tiffany's relationship came to an abrupt end,' Dom continued. 'Tiffany's gone into hiding, and the fact I'm facing my own legal troubles means shit to Mark's customers!'

'Well, they're all drug addicts, so that's not a surprise.' This was all I could say as I began to consider the possibility of cutting ties with Dom. I started pulling the Russian wedding ring on and off my finger.

In the weeks to come, I learnt Mark was charged with multiple accounts of supply and possession of Class A restricted substances. He faced his own criminal investigation. Unfortunately, Mark didn't make bail as he was uncooperative about who his associates were. Mark was a small fish in a pond of underworld drug dealers, and he feared retribution against his family.

'I've got a lawyer defending me,' Dom explained after giving me a rundown on Mark's situation. 'Actually, he's our family's attorney.'

'Why does your family have an attorney?'

'It's from way back. When I was a child and last in court, but for very different reasons. It was a compensation case. It was a case that resulted in me receiving $100,000 in cash upon turning eighteen years old.'

'$100,000?' I was blown away. 'What happened?'

'Sounds like a lot but I blew it in less than a year. Most of it was spent on my attempts to pretend I was straight.' The receiver of Dom's generosity was his fiancé, Sonya. Dom said he'd bought Sonya a premium diamond engagement ring that took up much of his compensation along with jewellery, make-up, cocktail dresses, and a holiday to Hawaii, where they did more shopping. Dom really had a pattern of trying to impress his love interests with material possessions. He'd obviously tried to impress me the same way. I wondered why Dom felt the need to overcompensate by doing so. The only thing Dom had bought for himself was a second-hand Mercedes that he'd later traded in for the Toyota that I recently wreaked. He had sold the Mercedes when money got tight living in Surry Hills and partying hard. I suspected the large sum of money Dom had come into at such a young age was what led him to have a taste for the finer things in life. It explained why he was foolish enough to fraudulently use a credit card just to have something new to wear to DCM.

'What was the money for?' I asked Dom after he explained nothing about why he got the money. 'Why did you get a compensation payout?'

'Don't want to say, Nathan,' Dom replied sternly and changed the subject. 'When are you coming back to Sydney?'

'Soon.'

'My lawyer wants me to see a psychiatrist,' Dom confessed. 'He thinks my best defence is to exploit my mental state at the time of the crime.'

'To do that, they need get to the bottom of what led you to your irrational actions?' I asked not even trying to mask my sarcasm.

'Mr Steel has a hunch my actions go beyond simply taking too many drugs and hanging out with the wrong crowd,' Dom agreed.

This is how my boyfriend found himself in another awkward interview situation, this time in a psychiatrist's room. Dom's fear at the prospect of going to prison and being raped lead the psychiatrist to prescribe Dom a course of legally mind-altering course of medications including anti-depressant, anti-anxiety, and anti-psychotic pills. Dom provided enough material for his lawyer to use in court and to be prescribed enough legal drugs to stop him from feeling how serious the situation he was in was.

~

With the second university semester complete, I returned to my parents' home and was reunited with Dom.

I asked Dom, 'Have you heard from Tiffany?'

'Nope.'

'When's the court case?'

'Next month.'

'You scared?'

'Fucking petrified. Can you imagine what would happen to a guy like me in prison?'

The thought of a handsome and openly gay twenty-one-year-old man like Dom being locked up with a bunch of hardened criminals raised the hair on the back of my neck.

Dom reflected on the last time he was in court. 'My dad was hit by a drunk driver when I was nine years old. I was the witness and had to testify in court about how many ice-creams cones dad had bought me, and from that they somehow worked out how much I should be awarded for the loss of my dad.'

'Oh my God!' I had no idea how disturbing my boyfriend's past was compared to mine. Finding out about Dom's past was one of the reasons I decided not to leave him or give up on him. In the process, I was reminded just how much my parents loved me. Not only did they fully accept I was gay, when I asked if it would be okay for Dom to move in with us, temporarily, they agreed without hesitating. I explained how Dom didn't get along with his mother.

'He'll only stay for a while, just long enough to find a new job and get back on his feet financially,' I promised.

'Okay. If that's what you want, Nathan,' my mum agreed, sounding fatigued. 'As long as it will help you both to stay out of trouble!'

Little did Dom or I appreciate, my parents' motivation and agreeing to this arrangement had more to do with keeping a closer eye on me. Because in mum's opinion, my boyfriend was a bad influence. One evening I overheard mum speaking to my nanna. 'I don't know what's worse, Nathan being gay or his criminal boyfriend.'

In the weeks before Dom's day in court, he was successful in finding employment as a telemarketer for a newly formed mobile phone reseller company called Quick Phones. Every dollar Dom earned, he spent on taking me out to clubs on Oxford Street, where we partied like there was no tomorrow.

We danced like we were dancing our very last dance. Knowing that, depending on the outcome of the impending court case, our relationship could change forever. It could go from the barrier of long distance to prison bars. We did the only thing that made sense. We took lots of drugs and grooved together under the laser lights until dawn, altering reality so that it seemed like nothing bad could ever happen to either of us, acting like Dom wasn't facing a jail sentence.

The experience of coming down in the spare bedroom of my parents' house, completely off our faces on acid, speed, and ecstasy, and pretending not to be wasted, felt like being high school boys again.

Dom and I giggled secretly to each other once we'd made it past my parents to seek refuge in my bedroom. Then we'd spend the rest of Saturday and Sunday mornings having comedown sex with the stereo on to cover our sounds, whispering to each other how awesome fucking each other felt. I never knew that it was possible to feel such intense passion or reach such heightened levels of ecstasy while on ecstasy.

It felt like a forbidden pleasure, knowing soon we wouldn't be able to have sex, depending on how things turned out. It was this knowledge that ensured we made every present moment count.

On the morning of his trial, Dom wore a navy-blue suit on his lawyer's advice. Blue was the colour of trust. My dad drove Dom to the Downing Centre Local Court building where the trial was set. In the back seat, I sat beside Dom and held his hand tightly. It had been agreed that I wasn't going to attend the hearing. Dom wanted me as far away from the trial as possible. He had already got me too deeply involved in his and Tiffany's stupidity. When Dad pulled up outside the court building, he ominously told Dom: 'You'll probably get a 3–5-year jail sentence.'

PARTNERS FOR LIFE

DOM WAS PUT on a 5-year good behaviour bond.

As the lawyer predicted, the Judge took into consideration Dom's troubled upbringing, how this effected his psychological state and ability to make sound judgements, plus the fact that he'd paid restitution to the bank, and was now employed full time again as a telemarketer.

The good behaviour bond came with a warning. If Dom stepped out of line and engage in criminal activity again, prison is where he'd find himself next. To celebrate Dom's freedom, we went clubbing and purchased illegal substances.

Neither of us considered for a minute the consequences of being caught using or buying drugs. For us, in the early 90s, scoring drugs was a normal part of clubbing and going out on the Oxford Street scene.

At DCM's first Foam Party, high on ecstasy, dressed in black shiny PVC pants and a mesh top, I kissed my free man. We were both covered head to toe in white soap suds. We stood in the middle of the familiar dance floor, which was turned into a make-shift tub filled with bubbles. It was the cleansing experience we needed to wash away the uncertainty of the last couple of months, a time in which our love had deepened to form a bond that we both knew would be a life-long connection. As the DJ played Rozalla's, 'Faith in the power of love', Dom stopped dancing in the waist-deep foam, pulled me close, and pressed his body against me.

'Thank you for standing by me!!' Dom yelled in my ear. 'I could never have gotten through it without you.'

I wrapped my arms around Dom's broad back and rested my head against his muscular chest. We were both covered in sweat. 'I'm grateful things turned out and you're free!' I yelled back. 'I don't know what I would have done if they sent you away.'

'Partners for life?' Dom asked me.

I looked at the shiny, ill-gotten, Russian wedding ring on my ring finger with hope. It reflected the flashing disco lights above our heads. 'Partners for life!' I agreed. Together we stood still, pulling each other close, both knowing how lucky we were. Knowing how close we came to being forced to separate.

As the techno beat intensified to 'Passion' by Gat Decor, the crowd packed on the dancefloor jumped up and down faster and faster to the music. Tiny clouds of foam floated around us. We started to laugh, releasing so much tension. The booming beats and soap suds made the adult night-club patrons smile like they were reliving their best childhood memories. Giant grins were illuminated with multi-coloured lights as green laser beams bounced off foam-covered skin.

~~

In the lead up to Christmas, I was overjoyed to find out I was successful in my application to transfer to The University of Technology Sydney. I took this as a sign from the universe that I was meant to be there for Dom, and to support him in the lead-up to the trial. I lost sight that it was also because I had the right stuff to be accepted into the BA Communication degree.

In the months following his sentence, Dom focused on re-establishing himself professionally. He was financially rewarded for becoming the top sales representative for Quick Phones. Thanks to the high commissions Dom earned for selling large bulky mobile phones to corporate clients, Dom gave me everything I could ever want, legitimately, from fragrances to designer jeans and t-shirts. There wasn't a CD I liked that Dom didn't buy for me. I didn't go wanting for anything.

Dom and I attended the major Sydney dance parties, like the New Year's Eve Sweat Party, and the Sydney Gay and Lesbian Mardi Gras after party for the very first time. It felt like a good time to be gay. The popularity of the Sydney Gay and Lesbian Mardi Gras was growing to a fever pitch, with the parade attracting over half a million spectators.

At Dom's work, everyone wanted to be his friend so they could get a ticket to the hottest *Members-only* party in town. I felt like the times were changing for the better for our community, and for Dom and me personally. This became apparent to me when my mum was more than happy to sew matching sequined outfits for her newly adopted gay son and I to wear to the Sydney Gay & Lesbian Mardi Gras after party. The silver outfits mum made with her Singer sewing machine were an expression of love. It was evidence that she didn't mind Dom and I continuing to live under her roof. In fact, she had come to encourage it. I think she was incredibly grateful to have me home after all the trouble I'd been lured into upon leaving the family home.

Her initial shock and disappointment at finding out her only child was gay had given way to acceptance, support, and custom-made matching flashy outfits which Dom and I wore with pride.

At the Mardi Gras after party, under a ceiling covered with suspended mirror balls, Dom and I experienced the euphoria that came from embracing one another for a kiss, without the slightest hint of shame, surrounded by our loving community and being with your one-and-only man. I had a sense of belonging I'd never experienced in my life. We were surrounded by people like us, knowing we had nothing to fear or be ashamed of for being gay. It was the best feeling in the world. It was the first time I felt that way. In the early 90s, Oxford Street and the gay scene was the centre of a beautiful alternate universe.

This was a world the masses previously had only gotten a thirty second glimpse of a year on the Sunday evening news. That was until now, as the parade was being broadcast on commercial TV. It was possible to watch footage of the Mardi Gras parade in all its glittering glory. While still going from the previous night's festivities, Dom ordered Chinese food as we settled in for an evening of spotting partygoers marching in the parade on TV. There was a sense of hope in the gay community that public acceptance of same sex couples was shifting in Australia for the better.

The following weekend, to thank my parents for their kindness, Dom took the four of us to Doyle's restaurant at Watsons Bay for a seafood lunch.

He had a lot to thank them for: the money they'd given him after the car accident, for opening their home to him, and not judging him over dragging their son into a criminal act. The lunch ended in an overly polite competition between Dom and my mum over who was going to pay the bill. It was no competition; Dom insisted it was only right that he showed my parents just how much they meant to him.

'It's a celebration,' Dom told my mum and dad. Both had their wallet and purse ready to pay the bill. 'Put those away! You've been more generous to me than anyone else has been in my whole life.'

'But, Dom, this restaurant is so expensive!' My mum sounded embarrassed. 'You should save your money! One day, you'll want to buy a home for yourself and Nathan, and that costs a lot of money now-days.'

I smiled at my mum's words. I suddenly felt like we were a completely new type of modern family, one I never dreamed could exist in Australia.

BETTER THE DEVIL
YOU KNOW

I N THE AUTUMN of 1992, I began attending lectures for the BA Communication degree at the University of Technology Sydney. Everything seemed to be coming together. I reflected on the past several months as though it had been a big test both Dom and I had had to go through to grow up and prove how much we meant to each other.

Unlike my first experience of university life in Lismore, at UTS I didn't look sideways at another male student, even though there was plenty to look at. This time, I was there to learn. However, thanks to my devotion to Dom, I partied each weekend in the bars and clubs of Oxford Street, far too hard to learn anything valuable covered in the lectures, apart from two things that stuck in my chemically-altered mind.

The first was the words from a burnt-out journalist holidaying as a stressed-out lecturer. Martin Freeman matter-of-factly informed his collection of aspiring journos' that the average life expectancy for a journalist was forty-five years due to the incredible job stress and the pressures meeting deadlines. This lesson turned me off wanting to pursue my dream of reading the news on TV.

The other comment that made an impression came from a media studies lecturer, who got through to most students sitting in the room when she advised, 'It should be your aim to become a critical thinker and to think of this course as a journey or a really good trip.' From that moment on, it became clear which students had popped acid trips as students shared knowing looks and giggled at the double meaning of the word *'trip'*.

A month into studying at UTS, I took a break on Sunday afternoon from writing an essay for the subject 'Media in Australia' and joined Dom who was washing his new pride and joy, a white BMW he had leased through work. As Dom rinsed off the suds from the hood, I popped out to join him on the driveway.

'Want a hand?' I smiled.

'Sure. Be a dear and get the vacuum.' Dom tilted his head to the vacuum supplies. I changed the nozzle on the Hoover to the bristle head and began absent-mindedly removing dirt and dust from the back seats. It was what the nozzle sucked up that made my heart skip a beat: two sets of matchstick packs stuck to the nozzle. The matchsticks were branded with the logo from KKK — Ken's Karate Klub in Kensington. It was the same gay sauna I'd once visited with John. Without saying a word to Dom, I flicked open each pack. To my horror, inside each pack were handwritten names, David and Andrew, with phone numbers.

I stood motionless. I thought about the possibilities of this discovery. When had Dom found the time to go to a gay sauna to meet other men, and to get their phone numbers? Dom and I had been having unprotected sex since I'd come back to Sydney. What if Dom had been unsafe with a bunch of strangers? My mind raced at the possibility that I could have been exposed to the HIV virus through Dom.

'What's wrong?' Dom asked, noticing I was frozen and looking like I'd seen a ghost.

'What's this?' I held up the matchstick packs.

'Don't know.' Dom shrugged nonchalantly.

'Have you been unfaithful?' my voice trembled.

'No.' From his voice, it was clear Dom had been caught out.

'Then what's this?' I asked in desperation.

'No idea,' he pretended not to know the truth. Lying to my face.

'How did these get in your car?' I yelled.

'How should I know?' Dom thought for a second. 'Maybe a client left it in there.'

'Bullshit!' I held onto the evidence and ran inside my parents' home. I raced to my bedroom, fighting the urge to cry from the hurt of realising my perfect life was nothing more than a facade. In my hands was evidence that my beloved boyfriend, the man I'd transferred universities for, the man who cost my parents a fortune and was enjoying the luxury of living rent-free, had obviously cheated on me.

'Nathan?' Dom raced into the bedroom and took me in his arms.

'You're an asshole!' I pulled away and glared at Dom. 'After everything we've been through, this is how you repay me?'

'It's not what you think!'

'Oh, really?'

'Let me explain.'

'When did you even find the time to go there?'

'Nathan, I won't do it ever again, believe me. I love you.'

'How can I believe you. You're such a good liar! I've seen you do it to my face before.'

I ran out of the bedroom and joined my parents in the living room. They both looked alarmed at the eruption of yelling they'd heard coming from the upstairs bedroom.

'Nathan, keep it down!' Mum scolded me. 'What will the neighbours think?' Mum closed the sliding door to our lounge room and garden outside.

'I want Dom out of here!'

'What's going on, Nathan?' Dad rose from his armchair, concerned.

'I can't tell you,' I grabbed the keys to Dom's BMW and headed for the driveway. Without thinking about how it would look driving a car partially covered in soapsuds, I got in, turned on the ignition and drove off. Let Dom explain to my parents what just happened, I thought to myself with hatred. That's all it would take for them to kick Dom out of their home. Hopefully, Dom would be gone by the time I returned home.

Before I knew it, I was driving erratically past Centennial Park. I tried to steady myself, not wanting to crash another one of Dom's cars. I drove towards Kensington, and soon found myself parked outside the same sauna from the matchsticks I found.

Kens.

I was in shock. I couldn't believe Dom had gone there behind my back. It was the ultimate insult and a betrayal of trust. After everything we'd been through, how could Dom do such a thing? I felt pure hatred for the man I loved.

I got out of Dom's car and crossed the road, determined to even up the score. It was the first time I had returned to Ken's since John had taken me there. Even though it was a bright sunny Sunday Sydney afternoon, inside Ken's it felt like midnight. It was dark, humid, and filled with an assortment of available naked men wearing nothing but white towels around their waists.

I wasn't too picky about who I led into a private cubicle. All it took was to make eye contact with another young half-naked man cruising by. With my heart filled with conflicting emotions, I kissed a young man, who was better looking than Dom, that I'd never seen before, on the lips. The stranger removed the white towel draped around my waist and began kissing my hardening cock. It was the first time I had sexual contact but felt nothing inside. I just went through the motions, enjoying the pleasurable act of sex. This was nothing more than a much-needed distraction from my own messed up life, a distraction from thinking things I didn't want to contemplate. Like how many times Dom had cheated on me and the possibility Dom had already given me HIV.

In the booth, I made sure the anonymous stranger and I used a condom. I didn't want to be responsible for passing on anything I could have already caught from my bad boyfriend.

⁓

It was getting dark by the time I returned to my parents' home. Mum and dad were visibly concerned.

'Where've you been?' Dad asked.

'Just out,' I sighed. I couldn't face them. I felt trapped, trapped in the home I'd grown up in. Upstairs, in my bedroom I found Dom. His face was a mixture of concern and alarm.

He looked startled to see me appear in the doorframe.

'I can't believe you're still here.' I rolled my eyes.

'Where did you go?'

'Where did *I* go?'

'We need to talk.'

'It's too late for that!' I felt deflated, my posture showed I just didn't care, not after having had sex with as many guys as my body allowed in one afternoon before exhaustion set in.

'Of course, it matters, Nathan. I love you!' Dom pleaded. 'You've got to believe me. I don't want to be with anyone else but you.'

'But yet you did. Do the names David or Andrew ring a bell?'

'Nathan, it won't ever happen again. I promise. You've got to trust me!'

'But I don't trust you Dom.'

Even though I had tried to screw away the emotional attachment I felt for Dom, the unfortunate truth was that I still loved this damaged soul. It was impossible to switch off the connection I had formed with Dom, especially after all we'd been through.

That night, Dom put his top salesman skills to use, trying to convince me not to end our relationship. He said things like:

We've been through so much together.

Give me another chance…just one more chance.

That maybe this is like the Kylie song, 'Better the devil you know'. We know each other so well that we should stay together.

As Dom promised he wouldn't do such a thing ever again, I just felt numb. 'How can I believe you ever again?'

'Because I mean it. You've got to believe me!' Dom rubbed my arm and looked deep into my tired eyes and spoke with complete sincerity.

'But I can't trust you anymore, Dom.' I looked deeply into his eyes. 'It's not like this should be a surprise. Tiffany told me you were a slut!'

'Tiffany's a bitch!' Dom tried to discredit my former best friend who'd gone into hiding. I now feared that the man I'd fallen in love with, the man I wore an ill-gotten ring from, who'd lied to my face, was a compulsive liar.

The following day, I told mum exactly what had happened the previous afternoon minus the gory sordid details. I let her know the reason Dom and I had fought was because Dom had cheated on me.

'No!' My mother sounded more disappointed about it than I had been. Being a country girl at heart, who'd been raised on a Queensland farm before moving to the city to marry the man of her dreams, my mother knew nothing about how the gay scene worked. She had no idea just how many other eligible young gay men lived in Sydney that would have been a far more suitable match for her son than Dom, men like Dan. It was this lack of knowledge that guided her response. 'But Nathan, you may never meet anyone else ever again.'

My mother's words played on my mind for weeks to come. At nineteen-years-old, I was naive and inexperienced enough to think that there was a chance my mother's advice could be true. That there was no way I'd ever be able to love someone else as deeply as I loved Dom. I should give him one more chance. I knew mum felt she was helping by encouraging me to stay with the young man she had also grown to love like a second son. Despite the evidence Dom had cheated on me and my instinct to cheat back, I decided to stay with Dom.

I couldn't leave him. I had formed a dangerous addiction to Dom. I gave Dom what he wanted: another chance. I hoped that there was some way we could repair our now unspoken 'open relationship'.

THE UNDERWEAR PARTY

AFTER DISCOVERING PROOF of my boyfriend's infidelity, I desperately hoped Dom would be true to his word and not cheat again. I was plagued with paranoid thoughts every time Dom wasn't with me. By the time I completed my final semester for 1993, Dom and I were talking about moving out of my parents' spare bedroom to make a fresh start.

To his credit, since the Ken's match box incident, Dom had continued to excel working hard at Quick Phones and spent all his spare time showing me the good life. They were make-up gifts, of sorts, Dom's attempts to repair the damage done through material possessions.

The first inkling I had Dom may be interested in more than me was when Dom came home all excited telling me we should attend Sydney's first official men-only underwear party.

'How do you know about this party?' I asked Dom with surprise.

'Sydney Star Observer.' Dom shrugged nonchalantly. 'It will be wild! Like Sleaze Ball on steroids.'

'Where's it being held?' I asked cautiously.

'At an old church on Cleveland Street in Surry Hills.' Dom grinned.

At twenty-one years old, I was conservative when it came to sex. I was monogamous. Dom was plenty of man for me. He was the only one I was interested in; despite everything he'd done. Yet now, Dom was interested in going to a party full of practically naked men. For a first time, I wondered whether I was enough for Dom. It began to dawn on me that, clearly, I wasn't. Dom was a one-on-anyone-he-could-get-on-the-side kind of gay.

Part of me was very curious to see what it would be like to dance all night with a bunch of men wearing only their underwear. 'Dancing in nothing but your underwear?' I clarified.

'Exactly!' Dom grinned.

'I think I'd be so embarrassed!' I laughed.

'You, my dear, have nothing to be embarrassed about!' Dom reassured me. 'Also, once you pop a disco biscuit, you'll be far from embarrassed.'

'Okay, let's do it,' I agreed.

In the week leading up to the Underwear Party, I pumped iron extra hard at the gym. After two years of working out at the Bondi Junction Fitness Network, I had sculpted a tight muscular body for a twenty-one-year-old man. Also, I spent fifteen minutes on a UV sunbed every second day. Every time, I came home a shade more tanned than the previous day my mother was annoyed.

'You'll give yourself bloody skin cancer if you keep it up with those damn tanning beds!'

But I didn't listen. Despite the bronzed and muscular reflection starring back at me in the mirror, as I did my bicep curls, I now wished that I'd been more receptive when the gym's complimentary personal trainer offered instant results by getting me on the juice. While I was all for recreational drug use, I didn't find the prospect of bigger muscles with a side effect of shrinking testicles a desirable trade-off.

Courtesy of my local beautician, Marilyn, at the New Elite Beauty Salon in Bondi Junction, I had perfectly smooth, hairless skin. Each month, Marilyn ripped every strand of dark arm, leg, chest, and stomach hair off my body with hot wax. To get through the torturous pain of my hair removal routine, I needed assistance that came in the form of codeine, which I took half an hour before each waxing session. I didn't think twice about washing down two Panadeine Forte pills with a miniature bottle of Drambuie before each wax. By the time I laid down on Marilyn's treatment bed, I was numb. Yet, even in this altered state, I still clenched my teeth each time Marilyn ripped a strip of body hair from my tight skin. I was prepared to suffer to achieve gay perfection. These were the lengths I went to ensure I looked like every other well-groomed young gay man on the Oxford Street scene in the early 90s.

Dom funded all these essential services. He also followed the same grooming routine to remain as smooth and golden as me. While my parents had come accustomed to the odd hours we kept on weekends while living under their roof, they were continually more horrified by our grooming decisions.

Dom and I thought my parents reactions were funny when they made such a fuss about the basics of gay grooming. Dom and I knew our routine was standard and essential, if not mandatory, to fit in and be part of the Oxford Street gay scene. Physical maintenance was necessary to ensure we had the confidence to strip down to our underwear and boots.

In the foyer of the old church, the line for the cloak room kept getting longer as gorgeous men took their turn to undress. Dom and I were eager to get a glance at the other men as they stripped down to their briefs. The challenge of this party was to keep it together as our drugs came on while we stood in line watching the free strip show unfold. We weren't the only ones checking out what the other men's choice of underwear was.

The atmosphere was charged with sexual excitement. Bursts of nervous laughter erupted from various men waiting to drop their gear and get down to their underpants. For many, like Dom and I, this was the first party of its kind where we had to strip before hitting the dance floor. When it was our turn, I felt a moment of stage fright. But when Dom grinned at me reassuringly, I flashed a cheeky smile in return and took off my clothes. In return for our clothes, we received a wristband to ensure we'd get our clothes back in morning. It was the *same rules as at Ken's*, I thought to myself as the chill of the night air touched my naked skin.

Inside the renovated church hall, there were over a hundred men, most of whom were in their twenties and thirties, and a few in their early forties. On ecstasy, I felt a sensation of love and being part of a community of survivors. There was an air of liberation in the hall. The crowd was beautiful, with virtually no body fat. The atmosphere was sensual and electric. It was a real-life version of a Michelangelo fresco filled with raw masculine sensuality. The air was charged as the DJ played 2Unlimited's song, 'No Limits'.

Dom and I danced close, but our eyes were glued to the sights of the other incredibly handsome men around us. Suddenly my heart swelled when I spotted two men I hadn't counted on seeing. In the corner of the room was my old university buddy Brad dancing with my former lover, Dan. Having taken the love drug, I smiled upon making eye contact and made my way through the barricade of beautiful bare backs, chests, and backsides towards the two men as Dom followed.

'What are you doing here?' I gave Brad hug and could feel his cock pressed against mine. 'Sorry, I didn't mean to touch it!'

'Relax, man,' Brad was wasted. 'We're all friends, right?'

'Right!' I grinned. 'I haven't seen you since Lismore. What are you doing in Sydney?'

'I moved back. And like I would miss this!'

'It's so good to see you!' I smiled.

Brad responded with a big kiss on the lips. To my surprise, I felt his tongue as we kissed. I responded by not letting go and pushed my tongue forward into Brad's mouth longingly. I'd always wanted to know what kissing Brad would be like. It was bliss. I didn't want it to end. In this environment, it felt like you could do whatever you wanted and get away with it. Just like a New Year's Eve party, at the Underwear Party, you could French kiss anyone if you had the right amount or chemicals in your system.

The kiss lingered as Dom watched on, acting cool. I realised Dom was turned on watching me and Brad kiss.

Dan and I made eye contact, and my heart stopped. He was still as handsome as ever. 'Hi, Dan!' I hugged him as a surge of desire shoot through my veins.

'I've missed you so much!' Dan whispered in my ear so Dom couldn't hear.

'Where've you been?' I asked.

'Living in London,' Dan explained. 'I've just come back to visit my parents.'

At first, I didn't know what to say as I felt my heart swell in response to Dan's deep voice. The feelings I once had for Dan unexpectedly flooded back with such intensity I held onto his back and didn't let go. I'd been storing these emotions somewhere deep inside within me. 'I should never have left your twenty-first birthday party,' I confessed.

Dan put his arms around me and gave me a hug.

All Dom could do was look on awkwardly. I think he was starting to feel left out. Suddenly, Dom did what he usually did when he felt threatened, he started dancing intensely to the music, jumping up and down to the rhythm.

'I wish you'd stayed that night too.' Dan didn't let me out of his lean and tight muscular arms. 'I'm leaving Australia next month to return to London. Want to come with me?'

'Yes!' Then I backtracked. "If things were different, yes. In a heartbeat,' I said in all seriousness. I didn't know if it was the ecstasy talking, making me so honest and unfiltered in my response. Suddenly, all I wanted was to be with Dan, forever. Seeing Dan again confirmed in my mind I was not with Mr Right. I suspected Dan was a one-on-one relationship type of guy, unlike Dom the man who'd cheated on me and now danced like a maniac.

In that instant, I caught Dom looking very uncomfortable and felt it was only proper to include him in my reunion with the two sexiest men I'd ever met. 'You remember my boyfriend, Dom?'

'Yes, unfortunately I do,' Dan replied, deliberately ignoring Dom.

'I can't believe you two are still together!' Brad shook his head in disbelief. 'Seriously, after that shit you guys got into. I thought that would be the end.'

'Thanks for that love. We're very much *still together*!' Dom gloated.

Brad told me he was now working as a fashion stylist and a part-time model on the side. He was also looking for a roommate. 'Do you know anyone who's looking to share?' Brad asked.

'We are! We're looking to move out from my parents' place.'

'Stop press! You're living with your parents? How does that even work?' Brad burst into laughter. 'Seriously, if you want to move in with me, that would be awesome. I'll even overlook that you're still inexplicably with Dom. Only because I've met so many weirdos since I advertised for a roommate. When can you move in?'

'Whenever you want.'

'Cool.'

'Where do you live?'

'It's a new complex on in Surry Hills called Roslyn Place.'

'Sounds lovely.'

'Oh, it is. Just think gay Melrose Place, and you've got it.'

When I told Dom I'd found a place for us to live, he was more than eager at the prospect of moving in with Brad.

'Move in with Brad?' Dom sounded excited. 'Sure!'

For the rest of the night, Dom couldn't keep his eyes off his soon to be flat mate's chest and abdominals. The four of us ran out of things to say and just danced together in only our underwear, all white, all Calvin Klein, all bulging.

Brad mouthed the words to Kim Sim's song, 'Too blind to see it'. He kept smiling at Dan and me. Dom's gaze glued to Brad's body distracted him from noticing how Dan and I couldn't keep our eyes and hands off each other, giving each other hugs for so many reasons. All it took was a smile and we'd hug lovingly making up for lost time.

Dan's eyes were filled with longing looks of desire while I wore an expression mixed with the dismay that came from wondering what could have been. 'Why didn't you pick me?' Dan yelled in my ear.

'I got sideswiped. I never meant to let you go!' I said looking over at Dom and realised his eyes were glued to Brad's crotch. Yet, it didn't bother me when I was high. In that instant, I came to peace with the knowledge Dom was never going to be faithful.

What finally tore Dom's eyes from Brad and my eyes from Dan was the sight of four well-known Albury barmen going from a passionate embrace to laying down on the floor as they ripped off each other's underwear. The men were grinding on top of one another, completely naked, without a care in the world as eager eyeballs watched with anticipation.

The Roman Gladiators of the Oxford Street gay scene were putting on a free show. It was a surreal experience, like watching a live sex-show unfold to a disco beat, a live hardcore porn version of Saturday Night Fever. Only John Travolta's character was nude and making out with several muscular men at the same time, men who were consumed with sexual desire and high levels of chemical confidence not to care who watched as they had sex on the dance floor.

Some men in the crowd cheered on at the dance floor orgy like they were at a sporting match. Barely a brief didn't have a massive erection.

DEBAUCHERY

MOVING OUT OF my parents' home to live with Dom in Surry Hills was the new beginning that we both needed. It was our chance to live the dream, a young professional and his university student boyfriend living with their male model roommate Brad.

On the day we moved in, we were greeted warmly at the entrance to the basement car park. Brad pressed the remote to let our white BMW through the automatic security roll-a-door.

'Welcome to your new home!' Brad gave me a hug as we stood beside the car. The boot was full of boxes filled with treasured possessions, designer brands, fragrances, ornaments, plus Madonna and Kylie CDs and LPs.

'Let me help you with these.' Brad grabbed a box of Madonna vinyl records and led us to the elevator. In the cramped elevator, we had an encounter with some familiar faces when it stopped on the ground floor. Dom's jaw dropped when he saw Aaron and Ricky enter, the same duo he once relied on to hide his and Tiffany's ill-gotten gains.

'Are you trying to hide more stollen goods?' Ricky flashed a cheeky grin directly at Dom.

'Ricky, that's no way to greet my new roommates.' Brad laughed, then turned to me. 'They're not stollen right?'

I shook my head with a grin.

'Roommates?' Aaron's brows rose with surprise before he flashed a smile at me. 'Boys, if you're not too exhausted from the move, swing by our place tonight. We're having an intimate party.'

'Sure, sounds good!' Dom nodded behind a box full of his belongings.

'Great. Pop by after eight,' Aaron said exiting the lift on the second level. 'Brad knows where we're at.'

'Welcome to the block!' Brad said once the elevator door closed. 'You don't have to go if you're not up to it. Trust me, there will be plenty more opportunities. Aaron and Ricky's intimate parties have started to blend into one another. I think it's business development for Aaron. They're always looking for new trade.'

'New trade?' I was curious what exactly Brad meant.

'You know, escorts?' Brad explained as the lift doors opened on the third floor. We followed Brad to our new shared apartment. Brad opened the door at the end of a beige corridor. The door revealed a large living room that had a nice balcony and view of the city skyline. It was an impressive sight. The view extended to our new bedroom. Dom and I were moving up in the world. In our new bedroom, we stopped for a minute to admire the view.

'Ready for a fresh start?' Dom's eyes were wide with possibility.

'I'd go anywhere with you,' I smiled back as Dom hugged me close.

'Time to christen the new bed!' Dom grinned and kissed me longingly, like he used to. Next, Dom pushed me onto the freshly delivered queen size mattress. The black wrought iron bedhead from Art of Stone bounced hard against the wall and rattled. We both laughed. Soon, we made the new bed rattle and squeak rhythmically as we settled into our new home. Fortunately, the concrete and brick walls were thick.

Once we finished having sex and unpacking our belongings, Dom and I were eager to explore the grounds and facilities of Roslyn Place. We wandered through the block to inspect an inner courtyard that had manicured gardens and was surrounded by balconies facing a large swimming pool in the middle.

'This is gorgeous!' Dom exclaimed.

His comment disturbed a group of young men sunning themselves by the pool. Upon hearing Dom's deep voice, the fit, tanned young men stopped talking and looked up. After the men observed Dom and I, they resumed their conversation.

'We were just seriously scoped,' I said under my breath.

'Like fresh meat!' Dom agreed.

Later that night, dressed in our most fashionable threads — sand coloured Caterpillar workmen's boots, Levi's jeans, and Morrissey Edmiston T-shirts — Brad, Dom, and I rang the doorbell to Aaron and Ricky's apartment.

'Come on in, bitches!' Ricky smiled, practically hanging on the door. It was only early evening but Ricky was wasted. He also looked very sexy wearing a tight red singlet and faded jeans. Ricky made a point of kissing each of us on the cheek. The apartment was the exact same configuration as Brad's, only the furniture looked more expensive and inside it was full of mostly older middle-aged men. As we entered, I could tell the men inside looked pleased at what they saw.

'Gentlemen!' Aaron greeted us each with a kiss and a hug. 'Glad you could make it.'

'We wouldn't miss one of your parties!' Brad flashed his Hollywood smile.

'Thanks for inviting us!' I smiled.

'Yeah! Thanks for inviting us,' Dom said. 'Feels just like old times.'

I didn't know what Dom meant when he said, *Feels just like old times.*

'Only better,' Aaron agreed. 'I'll introduce you to my guests in a second, but first, let me get you sorted with some champers.'

'Laced with speed!' Ricky whispered as he handed over three flutes of bubbly.

'Cheers!' The five of us clinked our glasses making sure we looked into each other's eyes for good luck.

'Let me give you the grand tour,' Aaron announced before showing Dom and I through his apartment. Along the way, he introduced us to other men who also lived in the apartment complex. First was a Brian, a lawyer, and his younger unemployed boyfriend Paul. They seemed friendly enough. Next were two men who lived together but weren't in a relationship. There was an older man named Ron who was dressed in a black leather waistcoat and assless chaps. He was wearing jeans, so his butt cheeks were fully covered. I forgot all my new neighbours' names immediately after meeting them thanks to my illicit champagne cocktail.

The tour ended in the master bedroom that had a very prominent wall hanging, a sleek black and white framed poster featuring a photo of Aaron and Ricky. They were both naked, posing so their legs were strategically covering their most valuable working assets: their crotches. In the image, their eyes looked directly towards the camera seductively. At the bottom of the poster was the logo of Sydney's premier male-to-male escort agency, Brett's Boys.

'Wow, that's some photo!' I blurted out.

'Nice shot.' Dom smiled and gave my butt cheek a squeeze.

It dawned on me that most of the older men at the party were probably clients of Aaron and Ricky's. Or *'trade'* as Brad had called it. Prostitution was how Aaron and Ricky managed to live in such a luxurious apartment and throw parties with free drugs for their neighbours. My head was spinning by the time I met the one person who didn't appear to be a client.

'Meet my fabulous new neighbour, Hazel!' Aaron announced with pride giving a middle-aged woman a sideways hug across her shoulders. Hazel looked a touch older than my mum. She had streaks of grey hair, wrinkles, and wore a smart black and white pants suit.

'Lovely to meet you,' Hazel smiled warmly. 'Where did you both live previously? I hear you're also new to Roslyn Place.'

'At my parents' home.' I smiled.

'His parents!' Dom cocked his head to my direction.

'This will be quite a change of scenery for you.' Aaron laughed and raised his glass to toast us joining the complex. Hazel laughed and looked like she was having the time of her life being the only lady in an apartment full of gay men. I suspected Ricky had neglected to mention to the more mature Hazel that her champagne contained speed when she announced, 'This is delicious. I'm on my third, and it has gone straight to my head!' That was probably a lot of speed for someone who I suspected had never tried it before.

Speaking with Hazel, Dom and I learnt she was a fifty-five-year-old and decided to live in the thick of it before she got too old to enjoy life. 'I'm recently divorced,' Hazel explained. 'I moved from the Northern suburbs into the city. I wanted a change from the dull life I was living in Dee Why.' Hazel spoke very fast. 'I raised two sons who never visit now they're all grown up, moved out, have kids and got on with their own lives.'

'Well, you're certainly living where all the action happens!' Brad joined us.

Hazel said she'd recently caught her husband cheating on her with her best friend. This revelation made my chemically altered mind rebound to the time I'd discovered the matchsticks from Ken's in Dom's car. The memory was never far from the surface.

'Also, after thirty years of marriage, once the kids had moved out, Jim and I simply ran out of things to talk about!' Hazel smiled as she took a sip of spiked champagne. 'Wow, this drink is really going straight to my head!'

From that point on, each glass of champagne blurred the reality of where Dom and I now resided with Brad. It was a gay wonderland of available men for a price, and a lady old enough to be their mother who was getting a big kick out of watching it all unfold unknowingly being spiked with speed.

'Isn't it dangerous to give a middle-aged lady these kinds of cocktails?' I took Ricky aside.

'She's loving it!' Ricky assured me and rolled his eyes. His pupils were enlarged and dilated.

'Hey, it's your party,' I reasoned somewhat dumbfounded.

Hazel left the party at 1am and commented that she'd loved every minute. I was just glad she didn't leave in an ambulance. I thought if Hazel were my mother, I'd be more upfront about what was in her drink and gain her consent. Then again, ignorance can be bliss.

By 3am, Dom and I realised we were the only ones left, apart from Aaron, Ricky, and Brad.

There was dance music playing, 'Dirty Cash (Money Talks)' by British dance music act the Adventures of Stevie V, the song took me back to when I had been clean and sober following the high school certificate. I considered how much I'd changed since then. Especially as Aaron, Brad, Dom, Ricky, and I'd somehow moved from sipping glasses of champagne laced with speed to snorting lines of cocaine directly off an ornate mirror. We each grinned at each other as the powder burned the back of our nostrils.

I was so wasted by 4am that I could no longer follow the meaning of the conversation being held by Aaron and Dom until Ricky abruptly announced something I did comprehend.

'I want to be fucked first!' Ricky's tone was eager. Aaron responded by fetching a bottle of amyl nitrate out of the freezer. He placed it on the coffee table and began unbuckling his belt.

'I think it's time to leave,' I whispered in Dom's ear, unsure about this turn of events. Even though I was wasted, I knew I didn't want to have sex with a prostitute, no matter how handsome they were. In my blurry state, I couldn't be sure what Dom and Aaron had negotiated to reach this point.

Were we about to have a fivesome?

Was it going to be free of charge?

Or were we going to pay for it later?

Welcome to the emerald city and suburbs surrounding the golden gay mile. What a way to get to know your neighbours, I thought with a mixture of apprehension and excitement through a disoriented state. I watched Dom pull his T-shirt off, stretching it over his head to reveal his broad shoulders and bare chest.

'Just relax,' Dom spoke in a soothing tone. 'It'll be fun.'

To my surprise, it turned out Ricky wasn't the first one to be fucked in the early hours of the morning. We all wore condoms.

~

'Thanks for welcoming us to the block!' Dom told Aaron before we returned to our new apartment.

'Thanks for coming. No pun intended!' Aaron winked. 'Just like *old times*.' Aaron's statement wasn't lost on me as he gave me a hug goodnight.

Later, when Dom and I'd wandered back to our new bedroom, I couldn't let what had just happened go without saying something.

'What were the '*old times*' like, Dom?'

'Pretty much like this. Private joke between me and Aaron.' Dom grinned. 'Let's just say back in the day, Aaron used to trade tricks with Mark for free pills. Tiffany never knew. Mark enjoyed being serviced on the side by the alpha male escort around town that is Aaron. I used to gladly join in!'

'How old is Aaron?'

Dom looked at me unsure. 'I don't really know. Thirty-something maybe. I don't think anyone knows.'

'Aaron's ridiculously sexy.'

'Funny, he said the same thing about you. Why do you think we waited until everyone had left the party?'

RIGHT IN THE NIGHT

WAKING UP WITH a throbbing hangover fuelled with alcohol, speed, and cocaine withdrawal, I wandered bleary-eyed into the living room at noon to find Brad eating a bowl of cereal and only wearing his black Speedos.

'Morning sunshine.' Brad grinned as he munched on a spoonful of corn flakes.

'Ouch!' I raised my hand to shield my eyes from the sunshine streaming in from the balcony. As I made my way into the kitchen to make some much-needed coffee, I heard snorting coming from Brad's bedroom. I glanced at Brad with curiosity.

'It's Ricky,' Brad explained with a knowing grin. 'His breakfast contains more chemicals than this cereal.'

'For breakfast?' My head hurt too much to comprehend the idea of starting the day with illicit substances. Then I considered the possibility that Ricky may not have slept yet, especially when he joined us in the living room and I saw the redness around his puffy eyes. Ricky rubbed his fingers under his nostrils and sniffled loudly. He was half naked, wearing only a white towel around his waist. My eyes immediately focused on the perfection of Ricky's golden-brown physique as he hung his arm around Brad's equally muscular shoulders.

'Hey, doll.' Ricky smiled at me clearly disorientated with his glassy eyes. 'Man! You got me going last night. Want to join us by the pool?'

'Sure!' I was getting to like Ricky.

'It's the only place to come down after a Sunday morning orgy.' Ricky grinned knowingly. I cracked up at this comment, somewhat self-conscious now I was no longer under the influence and had broken my group-sex virginity, free of charge. Yet again, regretting what I was coerced into doing while under the influence.

~○

The sounds of a distant disco beat could be heard from a nearby apartment. Jam & Spoon's, 'Right in the night' provided the perfect come-down soundtrack over the roar of rapid bubbles exploding inside the pool's large Jacuzzi. Enjoying the soothing bubbles, Dom rubbed my leg under the water as Ricky and Brad kissed each other. Aaron laid motionless and exhausted catching the afternoon sunrays by to the pool, along with a few other men.

Roslyn Place was a little gay oasis in the heart of Surry Hills. Then the serenity was disturbed by the sound of a loud mobile phone ring tone. The sound made all the men baking by the pool check the screen of their phones to see if the call was for them.

'Talk about a popularity contest!' I smiled.

'Yeah, to see who got the most trade from last night.' Dom chuckled.

The winner was Aaron, who placed his phone to his ear. 'Hello? Yes, I can do that. It's $200 per hour. In call or out call?'

'Guess I'll be spending the afternoon with you.' Ricky grinned at Brad.

'What a shame.' Brad smiled before pressing his lips against Ricky's.

'Hello, boys!' Hazel waved from the safety gate to the pool area. She was wearing a tasteful one-piece swimsuit with a blue silk-robe. To everyone's delight, Hazel was carrying a platter of fruit, green grapes, strawberries, and sliced banana with cheese and crackers she'd prepared especially for her new neighbours.

As Hazel joined us in the courtyard, Ricky smiled. 'Hazel, I wish you were my mum!'

'Aren't you a sweetheart!' Hazel blushed. 'But Ricky, you're far too young to be my son.'

'You know what will go with that platter?' Dom announced, getting out of the Jacuzzi. 'Champers!' Several minutes later, Dom returned to the pool and popped open a bottle of Moët he'd been saving as a housewarming gift. Dom poured the contents into several small plastic cups.

Suddenly, it felt like the previous night's party started up all over again as the men by the pool did their best to piece together vital details about the previous night, such as who had gone home with whom and what positions they'd engaged in.

KEPT MAN

THE FOLLOWING SATURDAY was World AIDS Day.

Aaron, Brad, Dom, Ricky, and I did our bit to help the cause by marching up Oxford Street to collect money for the Bobby Goldsmith Foundation. We carried red buckets asking for donations from the crowds attending the Shop Yourself Stupid fund-raiser.

That very night in the early hours of Sunday morning, international pop-star Belinda Carlisle rewarded the masses with a 4am performance at the Alexandria Stadium Summer Dance Party.

Belinda shouted into a microphone to the 4,000-strong audience, 'Fuck this jacket, and fuck these heals!' The audience responded with a roar of appreciation as Belinda tore off her denim jacket and kicked off her red stilettoes. One of the stilettoes landed back on her shoulder and the audience cracked up in laughter as Belinda launched into her hit, 'Summer rain.'

The crowd sang along in unison. For some elated partygoers, the lyrics moved them to tears. No doubt much of this audience had lost loved ones since the 80s and now the 90s.

Summer flew by, and soon it was time to attend The Sydney Gay & Lesbian Mardi Gras after party. No one on the massive dance floor knew what to make of the sight of Aaron bringing Hazel onto the emptying dance floor at 5am. The revellers couldn't believe what their dilated pupils were seeing, including Hazel, who loved every minute of the experience. To an outsider, it looked like Aaron was bringing his mum to the biggest disco in town.

'You're never too old to go to a Mardi Gras after party!' Aaron yelled in Hazel's ear.

'Thank you, sweetheart. You're like the son I never had.' Hazel smiled. 'This is so wonderful!' Hazel grinned and clapped her hands to the booming house music beat of Martha Walsh's 'Carry on'. It looked like it was such a thrill for Hazel to be there with her newly adopted gay foster children as the Roslyn Place club kids danced with the block's newly appointed mother figure. We were more than friends. We were one big happy family. Watching Hazel's smile under the disco lights made me wish I could take my parents to the afterparty. But I knew they were too square for this kind of action. I suspected what Hazel had lived through made her more open to trying new things. She had a different perspective on life. Hazel had achieved her mid-life goal of getting closer to the action and living her life to the fullest.

'Never in my wildest dreams did I imagine I'd get to enjoy this stage of my life this much!' Hazel smiled gratefully.

Thanks to Aaron, Hazel joined the partygoers who migrated, wearing dark sunglasses, to the laneway behind the Beresford Hotel the following morning to continue partying.

'Hazel this is what we call a recovery party!' Aaron explained as he introduced her to a laneway full of people dressed in very little clothing and drinking beer at 9.30am.

By this point in time, nothing made much sense. The unofficial competition for 'last man or lady standing' had begun. It was obvious that all the revellers were taking an increasing range of substances to stay upright. But not all people could cope mentally with consuming so much illicit chemicals coupled with sleep deprivation and alcohol.

This became obvious when a very skinny, middle-aged man covered in body glitter approached the Roslyn Place club kids. The poor soul was shaking and looked terrified. 'Do…you…have…any…Valium?' The stranger looked like he was going to fall apart from nervousness.

'Sorry, doll,' Dom answered as sympathetically as he could. It was a harsh reality seeing someone reacting so badly to having consumed too much and not knowing when to head home.

The man looked horrified at Dom's response and mumbled, 'Thank… you,' before he disappeared into the crowd.

'Well, that was a downer.' Ricky frowned.

'Some people just don't know when enough is enough!' Brad shook his head.

'If I ever get like that, take me home!' I instructed Dom.

'Okay, we'd better get you home. Shall we?' Dom joked and gave me a loving hug.

Since Dom and I moved into Roslyn Place, it felt like our lives had become one long endless bender. When there wasn't a major dance party on, nights were spent inside the Midnight Shift before recovering by the Roslyn Place pool. If the boys weren't recovering by the pool, Dom drove Aaron, Brad, Ricky, and I to spend the day working on our tans at Tamarama beach, or as Aaron called it, 'Glamarama'.

'Glamarama! It's where all the people you saw out last night are now passed out and sunning themselves during the day.'

'Yeah, its Oxford Street by the sea,' Brad agreed.

As we made our way across the hot sand, Aaron couldn't help but joke under his breath, 'Client...client...client...,' while nodding his head discretely at various men who were baking in the sun. I couldn't believe how many men Aaron claimed were *clients*, especially the men sunning themselves with young ladies who looked like romantic couples. But in Sydney, who could tell who was straight anymore?

For a bit of variety, Aaron suggested we join him in visiting the nudist beaches that were popular with many gay men such as Lady Jane at the South Head and Obelisk on the North side of Sydney Harbour.

'Trying to drum up more trade?' Brad joked.

'It always about the trade,' Ricky agreed.

'Just think of it as advertising.' Aaron shrugged as he pulled down his boardshorts to reveal his semi-swollen penis while we strolled past naked men sunning themselves on the pristine shoreline. Most had their eyes on Aaron's prize.

It was at the local nudist beaches where I discovered it was common knowledge that casual sex just happened behind the rocks of the shoreline or in the bushes in broad daylight. Everyone knew exactly what was going on when a man casually wandered into the bushes or behind the rocks, completely naked. It was all part of the free entertainment in the harbour side city.

Before leaving the nudist beach late afternoon, Aaron caught the eye of a Gilligan's barman and Aaron excused himself from his boyfriend, Ricky. Ricky watched on as the two men followed each other into the woods together.

'Ricky, is your man some kind of sex-addict?' I asked.

Ricky didn't answer me.

I couldn't believe how easy it was for strangers to have sex with a male escort without having to pay for it. Like when we stayed back after Aaron and Ricky's party, it was not on credit. For Aaron sex was his sport. He was very competitive.

'Aaron sure has stamina,' Dom said knowingly as I noticed Ricky looked momentarily insecure waiting for Aaron to return from the bushes.

When I returned to university tutorials after the summer break, I had the apartment all to myself to study. Most of the time, I studied by the Roslyn Place pool. On weekdays, I enjoyed the experience virtually all to myself, apart from the occasional prying eyes of the other men who didn't work in conventional 9-5 jobs, such as the local DJ, drag queen, and barman who checked out the sight of me only wearing red Armani Speedos from their balconies overlooking the pool.

I developed a routine that consisted of a morning workout at the local Fitness First Network gym on the next block followed by a quick swim and sunbake before midday. This was followed by eating a light ham sandwich for lunch and a hurried walk through the long, tiled tunnel underneath Central Station that led to Broadway to attend afternoon lectures at UTS. With Dom and Brad paying the rent, in an odd way, I felt like I had unwittingly become the very definition of a kept man.

It also became apparent that I had become the envy of the other kept men who resided at Roslyn Place, such as Ricky, who joined me poolside to sunbake every now and then.

'So, you don't work at all?' Ricky sounded a touch envious.

'Nope,' I answered enjoying the morning sun. 'I'm doing a degree.'

'La-de-da!' Ricky frowned. 'Sounds dull.'

'For some.' I tried to hide my annoyance at Ricky's remark and changed the topic. 'So how long have you and Aaron been together?'

'Since I was sixteen. My parents threw me out when they found out I was a homo. I was living on the streets and working The Wall until Aaron took me in.'

'I had no idea; that's so harsh! Ricky I'm sorry you had to go through that!' I was taken aback, reminded not everyone had parents as understanding as mine when it came to *coming out*.

'Aaron really is a good guy, isn't he?'

'Sure is. Just like Dom!' Ricky turned his stocky body over on his towel to sun his back. 'You're lucky you have Dom!'

'No, Ricky, it's the other way around. Dom is lucky to have me.' I felt it important to assert myself on this subject.

'How so?' Ricky scoffed, confused by what I'd said adding. 'Dom could afford to have any toy boy he wants.'

'*Toy boy*. He could?'

Until this point, I had never seriously considered myself to be a *toy boy*.

However, being the only other young man apart from Ricky having the luxury of sunning himself by the Roslyn Place pool on a Wednesday morning, I could appreciate how I could be mistaken for nothing more than Dom's *toy boy*. For a second, I considered the prospect that Ricky could be thinking of making a move on my man, wanting to upgrade to a newer model named Dom. There weren't many men who could fill Aaron's role to pay for Ricky's drug habit and maintain his lavish lifestyle. Aaron paid for Ricky's gym membership, clothes, and $200 haircuts in Paddington. I'd found out how outrageously expensive Ricky's haircuts were when Ricky had insisted on taking me with him to get my hair dyed blue black by Ricky's stylist, Dean.

To my surprise, Ricky introduced me as, 'Meet Nathan, he's my new best friend.'

'I like him a lot better than the last one, love!' Dean commented as he sniped off a piece of my fringe.

'That's what you said about Greg!' Ricky snapped.

'I know, but this one is way cuter!' Dean winked at me in the mirror.

I was flattered and a little disturbed. I didn't like being referred to as 'this one', and I wondered whatever happened to 'the last one'? As Dean styled my hair, I began to wonder about how many 'new best friends' there had been for Ricky before I'd come along. Ricky's words about Dom being able to 'afford any toy boy he wants' played on my mind for weeks. As did Dom's private joke, 'Just like old times.'

After all, Dom was earning higher and higher commissions selling an increasing number of mobile phones to the top end of town. This was evident from regular shopping sprees to buy countless vinyl club remixes from Central Station Records, posh fragrances, as well as dining out at the best restaurants in town. Not to mention the endless supply of drugs when we went out dancing. My contribution to the relationship was sexual. Most mornings before Dom left for work, Dom liked me to sit on his dick. But what separated me from Ricky in my mind was the knowledge of everything Dom and I had lived through to reach this point. If anything, Dom still owed my dad $30,000. Also, he owed over a years' worth of rent that he conveniently never offered to pay. Not that my parents expected him to. They were just trying to keep me out of trouble.

Also, I was lucky that I could go home to my parents at any time if I needed, and didn't require the support of another man. Plus, once I graduated with my degree, I would get a decent job and would make good money on my own without having to sell my body. I wasn't judging Ricky. I knew I was going to follow a different path to make a living. I was sure once I graduated, I'd contribute an equal financial component to my relationship with Dom.

In the meantime, I nonchalantly embraced my newfound status as a toy boy as my life morphed into a haze of university lectures and late nights clubbing and partying.

Life at Roslyn Place became sketchy in so many ways.

Each weekend started with Thursday Night Shopping at DCM, then Friday nights drinking Berry Fabulous, Oxford Smashes, and Long Island Ice Teas at Gilligan's over Taylor Square. Saturday nights was all about dancing at the Midnight Shift and Sunday nights were back at Gilligan's for more cocktails.

Hanging out with Aaron, Brad, Dom, and Ricky, I never had to join a line to get in an Oxford Street venue. We were always waved through by the door staff, straight past the line of patrons waiting as if we were local celebrities. It never occurred to me that by hanging out with two of the town's most prominent male escorts, people who didn't know me just assumed I was the latest call boy on the gay scene as was Brad.

This became clear when a stranger approached me in the tiny men's room of Gilligan's. The well-groomed middle-aged man asked me, 'What's your rate?'

Being drunk and intoxicated, I thought the question was hilarious. 'You couldn't afford me, honey,' I replied, exiting the men's room.

Later, when I bragged about the encounter to Dom, he looked annoyed rather than amused and wanted to know which older man had asked the question within the packed cocktail bar.

'Frightened I'm going to leave you for a richer older gentleman, hey?' I teased.

'Just don't get any ideas.' Dom grinned strangely.

It didn't take long before the idea of being a *kept man* soured severely for me when Aaron joined me by the pool as I sunned myself before lectures. 'You know you remind me of me when I was your age.'

'How so?' I asked, intrigued.

'For starters, I came from a nice middle-class home. Also, when I was younger, around your age, I was at University of Sydney and a kept man.'

'I'm not really a kept man Aaron.'

'Oh, really?' Aaron said sarcastically. 'Let's do the math. Who pays your rent? Who takes you shopping? Who buys your drinks and who takes you out to eat?' I said nothing as Aaron listed these activities and waited for me to react. Since there was no reaction, Aaron continued, 'I'm just making a comparison. It's a compliment, if you can pull it off the way you seem to be doing. Nothing wrong with what you're doing, but just know, as you get older, the hours of being kept will grow shorter and shorter until you find yourself charging an hourly rate. Like me.'

'I highly doubt it, Aaron! I'm not like you. When I get my degree, I will have a professional career very soon!'

'So, did I. I have a BA in Philosophy tucked away in my filing cabinet somewhere. I just found an easier way to make a living than the one I studied for.'

'How philosophical of you,' I responded before ending the conversation by diving into the blue chlorinated water. The cool water soothed my discomfort at the idea of what my loving neighbours predicted my future would be like.

SMOOTH AEROBICS BODY

SINCE MOVING INTO Roslyn Place and unintentionally becoming a *kept man*, I was continuously amazed by how many men seemed to know Dom quite well when we were out. However, I didn't know who any of these attractive men were. They would smile at Dom like they knew him, intimately.

But they never said a word to me. They acted like I didn't exist. It was like they were letting me know not very subtly they had no interest in me; they wanted to get past me to speak to Dom. The handsome strangers who acknowledged Dom had one thing in common. They were all members from the Fitness First Network gym evening classes, the ones I didn't attend because I had university lectures.

Ricky let the cat out of the bag one morning as we sunned ourselves by the pool. 'Dom has developed quite a reputation among the boys who do aerobics classes at Fitness First Network. They know Dom, not from the aerobics floor but the gym's other facilities, if you get what I mean!' Ricky chuckled. 'Dom's one of the gym's main attractions. I've heard in the darkness of the steam room is where all the action happens!'

'Don't bullshit me, Ricky!' I pretended I wasn't hurt by this revelation. 'You're kidding, right?'

'Doll, from what I hear, Dom regularly plays a game of hanky panky with the boys' once they've finished *the grapevine.*'

Even though I sensed something was going on each time an attractive stranger said hello to Dom and ignored me, I told myself I was just being paranoid, that it was the drugs making me think suspicious thoughts, that there was no way Dom would cheat on me again. Not after 'Ken's. But I couldn't ignore what Ricky had to say. For some reason, I knew in my heart Ricky was probably right. I could also tell Ricky enjoyed stirring up trouble when he was bored, which was most days. With friends like Ricky who needed enemies.

'I'm just trying to help,' Ricky shrugged his shoulders. 'At least you know babe.'

I didn't want to believe what Ricky said was real, or that it was happening all over again. Only now on a completely new level.

'Why would Dom cheat again now?' I asked Ricky, desperate for an answer.

'Because he can,' Ricky raised his brow. 'If you haven't clocked it, Dom's giving signals he's ready to trade you in for a newer model. Many of the contenders are laughing behind your back.'

The timing of Ricky's words was frustrating as there was no way I could confront Dom. Dom was away in the Gold Coast, on business. Or so Dom had said. Now, I didn't know what was real or fake. Dom was allegedly at a conference for being one of the top sales performers at his company.

My heart raced when I tried to phone Dom's mobile and I received an automated message that his mobile phone was switched off. I began to wonder if there was really a conference on. Or was Dom somewhere else with someone else? Was he with one of the boys that ignored me but said hello sweetly to Dom.

To compound the issue, there was a mysterious person who rang our home phone line only to hang up the second I answered. I was meant to be working on my Film and Gender Identity assignment, but instead, my mind was in over-drive about the *identity* of the mysterious caller. They kept calling on the hour, waiting, checking. It was like being in that scary movie, 'When a stranger calls'.

The fifth time the phone rang, and the caller hung up when I answered, I was certain Dom was doing the dirty behind my back again. The mysterious caller was probably one of Dom's latest flings. There was no other explanation.

I was so unsettled. I paced the apartment back and forth, resisting the temptation to go snooping through Dom's things.

After being hung up on for the seventh time, that night, I found myself obsessively going through Dom's belongings: his briefcase, his clothes drawer, his clothes, and finally his gym backpack. I was trying to find proof and check there was no evidence of Dom cheating on me behind my back. Inside an internal gym backpack zipper pocket, I found something I was not emotionally prepared to discover.

On a small piece of yellow Post-it Note was a distinctive phone number and a passcode written in Dom's handwriting. Staring at the square yellow paper, I felt physically ill holding what I knew was most likely the details of a sex chat line membership. Now I knew how my mother must have felt all those years ago when I was sixteen and she'd discovered my gay porno magazines: sick to the stomach.

Vertigo set in. The bedroom closed in around me and I couldn't breathe. There was only one thing left to do. I couldn't resist dialling the number. Within seconds, I was connected to an automated sex chat line and a recorded man spoke with an Entertainment News correspondent worthy tone.

"Welcome to Guys for Guys, the hottest men ready for action, just a phone call away. Please enter your passcode now!"

I punched in the passcode I'd found in Dom's gym bag and was given a set of instructions, one of which was the option to review your own profile message. My heart pounded hard in my chest. I did as the recorded message instructed and pressed 7 to listen to Dom's profile.

"Hi guys," Dom sounded distant and nonchalant. "I'm Dom—"

My jaw dropped. I couldn't believe Dom had had the balls to use his real name.

"I'm a good looking twenty-four-year-old guy, six feet five inches tall, with a thick eight-inch cut cock, and a smooth athletic body. I'm looking to hook-up for a good time."

I played the recorded message over and over and over. I was in disbelief that Dom had resorted to advertise for hook-ups behind my back while pretending to be in a committed relationship. After the fifth time that I'd listened to Dom's profile message, I decided to leave Dom a message of my own. There was only one response I could think of.

'Hi, I'm Nathan. I'm a twenty-three-year-old guy who is tall, dark, and has a tight, muscular, gym-toned body, and by the time you hear this message, Dom, you'll be single. You're dumped!'

With those words, I hung up and let out a shaky breath. Tears welled in my eyes. How long had this been going on?

I couldn't wait for Dom to retrieve his messages from Guys for Guys. I was in disbelief this is what our relationship had come to after four years. It was to end on a tacky phone sex chat line. It was so impersonal, mechanical, modern. There was only one thing left to do. I began packing my belongings.

It took a few hours to pack up my stuff, including my Apple Mac computer. By the time I was done, I heard the front door open. It was Brad.

'What's going on?'

'I'm leaving!'

'What happened?' Brad's tone indicated he already knew exactly what might have happened.

I didn't say a word. I grabbed the Post-it note, picked up the phone, dialled the 0055 number, punched in Dom's passcode, and handed the phone to Brad.

As Brad listened, a smirk spread across his face and his eyes lit up. 'Oh my God!' Brad grinned, and he pressed 7 to listen to the message one more time before bursting into laughter. Brad bent over he laughed so hard. Seeing the hurt in my eyes, Brad tried to contain his amusement. He did not do a very good job of it. 'I'm sorry, Nathan,' Brad apologised. 'But this is just too funny!'

Brad's advice many years ago had been to dump Dom, and that Dom was vile. This vividly ran through my mind. Brad had been a good judge of character.

Realising how seriously hurt and humiliated I was, Brad put his arms around me. 'Gee, Nathan, you were with someone who has a '*smooth aerobics body*' and none of us even knew it! I mean, let's face it, it's not like Dom has ever had a smooth aerobics body since you met him. In fact, since he's been living here, Dom has seriously porked out!'

Brad's bitchy observation made me smirk and feel slightly better about my decision to dump Dom on *Guys for Guys*.

'Do you want a Valium, doll? You really look stressed,' Brad kindly offered.

The following morning, back at my parents home, I got a phone call from Dom in the afternoon.

'Very funny.' Dom sounded unimpressed.

'Is that seriously all you have to say?' I was amazed at his audacity to not even say hello or sorry. Just 'Very funny.' What a heartless person Dom had grown up to be.

'What do you expect me to say?' Dom put on a sarcastic voice. 'Please, don't leave me, Nathan. We're meant to be together.'

'Why are you using a phone sex line? Aren't I enough for you?'

'It's not that. I don't know. I was just curious. I never met anyone from that line.'

'Oh, really? Just like you never met anyone at Ken's?'

'Baby, it's the truth!'

'Don't call me *Baby* and don't you get tired from constantly lying?'

I suspected Dom was only concerned about what I would tell our collective friends about my discovery. He was probably frightened they'd react as Brad had, with uncontained amusement. But that was the last thing I cared about. I had no intention of telling anyone else. It was all too humiliating. It was hard to face the reality I'd been so unaware and blind to what was going on. I was at university. I was a smart person. Why was I so dumb and hopelessly in love? I thought I had been living the high life, living in the fast lane. Somehow, I'd gotten addicted to the lies.

'I swear, Nathan, you're the only one for me. I just fucked up. Please come back. You know we're made for each other! Nathan, you complete me! I'm sorry, baby!' Dom pleaded. I couldn't listen to the lies any longer and hung up without saying another word.

Spending Sunday afternoon alone at my parents' home, typing up an essay on the negative portrayal of homosexual men in Hollywood films, I couldn't get Dom off my mind.

I couldn't reconcile why I still loved Dom so much despite all he'd done. I began to wonder if it was misdirected love to fill the void left by my first same-sex love, at the age of sixteen, Campbell, a man who had disappeared off the face of the Earth. A man I thought about often. Dom and Campbell were physically similar types: tall, built strong, and hung. They were every gay man's fantasy, the straight-looking footballer type.

I started to wonder if I had an undiagnosed mental health problem and decided to book a session with a psychologist. I saw a lady named Rachael, who gave me a book to read called, 'The dance of anger'. It was all about women trapped in abusive and toxic relationships.

Rachael told me, 'In your case, I think you'll find it very useful to help understand the cycle of abuse you've been caught in. It's a dance, and you need to change how you move in relation to Dom.'

By the following week, I missed Dom so badly I decided to move back in with him and accept his half-baked apology. Full of conflicting emotions, I was ready to start the dance all over again. Just as the book said that women caught in my situation did. I didn't trust Dom an inch, but at the same time, I felt like I couldn't live without him.

I didn't want to leave Dom because I couldn't imagine going out on the Oxford Street scene without him. My self-confidence had reached an all-time low. I'd become so co-dependent I couldn't picture my life without my poorly selected Mr Right.

Upon returning to Roslyn Place, Dom threw me on our queen size bed where we made aggressive make-up sex. Raw, passionate, and unprotected love. As I let Dom enter me, I hoped I hadn't already contracted something fatal. Next time, I promised myself, *we'll use condoms.* I knew things had to change. From now on, I had to change the way I behaved in relation to Dom. I foolishly told myself that our relationship was going to be on my terms, not Dom's. If Dom seriously wanted me to be *his boyfriend,* there would be no more unsafe sex. If Dom wanted to have unprotected sex, it would have to be with someone else.

I didn't like the idea of Dom getting it on the side, but I came to accept that Dom was incapable of being faithful.

In the coming months, I got my revenge. I used the same Guys for Guys phone sex chat line to meet random men and returned to Ken's sauna, alone. Meanwhile, Dom and I did our best to pretend to each other that we were faithful. We enthusiastically agreed that we would spend the rest of our lives together, that we'd always be together, just the two of us.

However, I knew Dom and I were getting talked about for all the wrong reasons. Ricky and Brad told me that Dom and I were the talk of Roslyn Place because our relationship was so tragic.

Proof of this fact was since accepting Dom was not being faithful, I began getting tested for HIV and STIs monthly.

YOU'RE STILL
WITH THIS GUY?

ARON LOOKED LIKE he was in no mood to celebrate the fact he was getting older at the surprise birthday party Ricky held at their apartment. That's why, on the night of his fortieth birthday, Aaron disappeared from his own party. I don't think Aaron liked that Ricky had highlighted that fact Aaron was now officially middle-aged. It was bad for business. Brad and I suspected Aaron had fled his party to pursue his preferred method of celebration: being on a cocktail of drugs and fucking similarly minded men at Ken's.

Aaron's absence from his own birthday celebration soon left his guests wondering where he was. As Brad and I scanned the room looking for Aaron, I spotted something else that disturbed me to my core. I caught a glimpse of Dom talking to a group of men that I didn't recognise, apart from Ricky. As I watched Dom, I saw him casually feel up another guy's ass while we were both in the same room.

Dom noticed me looking in his direction and he simply pretended his hand wasn't squeezing another man buttocks. Dom waved to me with his other hand. He acted like nothing was happening right in front of my disbelieving eyes. My heart sank. Dom's hand had been squeezing Ricky's ass. I looked at Brad who was also looking in the same direction. Brad just shrugged nonchalantly and took a sip of champagne.

I didn't care anymore what Dom did behind my back. Yet, when it came to his public behaviour, especially if I was present and it was with someone we both knew, who lived in the same apartment complex and was a prostitute, this threatened what was remaining of my sanity.

Being drunk and a little high, I didn't know what to do in response to this turn of events. Should I confront Dom at the party and make a scene or wait till later? Initially, my response was to pretend I saw nothing. I was my mother's son. I preferred to live in denial.

When I looked back again, I realised something was up. Dom and Ricky had left the living room and were headed for the bedroom. I followed cautiously only to see the bedroom door close. My heart sank. I was hyperventilating as I grabbed the door handle and aggressively pushed it open. I barged in to find Dom and Ricky in an intimate embrace on the bed.

Dom and Ricky both looked startled to see me in the doorway, having been caught out. They both said in unison, 'What?', while wearing guilty expressions.

This was a turning point. I had taken all I could from Dom's psychological abuse, abuse I had come to accept as normal. The lavish lifestyle wasn't worth the emotional turmoil and uncertainty. Our dance of anger was done.

I had a flashback to the words the Lismore university psychologist once asked, *'And you're still with this guy?'* I stormed out of the bedroom to find Brad drinking with Hazel. 'Can we get out of here?' I was holding back the urge to burst into tears. My whole body was trembling.

'Sure!' Brad led me into the bathroom. Hazel followed, not wanting to miss the drama. Once we were all in, Brad locked the door and looked concerned. 'What is it?'

'Dom is cheating on me with Ricky!' I broke down and fell into Brad's arms. Brad patted my back, and in the mirrored walls I could see Brad's awkward expression as he looked at Hazel somewhat confused.

'I know!' Brad confessed in a caring tone. 'It's been going on for a long time.'

'It has?' I pushed Brad away in a state of shock.

'We all thought you knew!' Brad seemed surprised. 'Why do you think I stopped dating Ricky?'

'I had no idea!' I wiped away tears and left the party.

Hazel called after me, 'Love he's not worth it! You're better than him, dear!'

My whole relationship with Dom had become an exercise in cruelty.

'Damn it!' I cursed. Why didn't Dom value my commitment to him? Wasn't I a good toy boy or whatever I was to Dom? Since the night we'd met, Dom had become my whole world. I'd left Dan for Dom. What a huge mistake.

When I returned to our apartment, I began throwing my clothes into a suitcase, all the fancy clothes Dom had bought for me. This time, I was going to leave Dom and never come back. There was nothing Dom could say to salvage this mess. As I closed my suitcase, I heard the front door open.

'What are you doing?' Dom's large physique blocked the bedroom door.

'I'm getting out of here.' I couldn't look Dom in the eye. I was still crying.

'You'll never meet anyone as good as me ever again!' Dom sounded cocky.

'That would be just fine,' I snapped.

'You can't leave me!' Dom slurred his words.

'Dom, we're over. I've had enough.' I felt numb. I was disappointed in myself that it had taken this long to work up the courage to stand up to Dom and accept the real nature of our relationship. The knowledge that Dom had been cheating on me with Ricky was too much to contemplate.

'Trust me, Nathan. We're not over!' Dom warned.

'Trust you?' I almost laughed as tears blurred my vision. 'There is no trust in this relationship.' I tried to push past Dom, who was still blocking the bedroom door. 'I'm leaving.'

'No, you're not!' Dom grabbed me aggressively by my shoulders. He faced me with an intense stare as his cheeks turned red. 'You're not leaving me. You belong to me.'

Dom's tone was frightening. I struggled to escape his strong grip. Dom had extra height, weight, and strength over me. Being high on drugs, I felt helpless and realised I was physically trapped.

'Let me go, you bastard!' I tried to push myself away from Dom's chest.

'You're not fucking leaving me!' Dom repeated in a disturbingly low tone.

I squirmed to free myself. 'You don't deserve me. I never want to see you again.'

Dom released his hands, and I was free. That's when Dom landed a punch on my chin. The blow was so hard that I bounced back. Everything went black for a few seconds; I was in shock. My ears were ringing as I came to. I found myself wrapped in Dom's muscular arms.

'I'm sorry!' Dom embraced me, rocking gently and repeating the words. 'I'm so sorry. So sorry.'

I froze in a state of shock. What was worse was that I could feel Dom's dick hardening against me as I allowed myself to be comforted by my abuser. To compound my sense of confusion and betrayal, I also became aroused and responded with a raging erection. Dom interpreted this as a free pass to kiss the man he'd just beaten.

Drugged, disoriented, and confused, I didn't stop it, feeling hate and lust at the same time as passion took over. Soon, we were naked on the carpet having hard, violent, and primal make-up sex. It was the most intense fuck we'd ever had. It was desperate and filled with conflicting emotions. With each thrust, I couldn't believe I was allowing this to happen again.

All along, I wanted to be loved. I'd been cheated on, abused, beaten. I knew this wasn't how love was meant to be. I knew I had to leave. I just couldn't do it with Dom inside me.

I didn't sleep at all that night. Anxiety kept me awake. As soon as the sun rose, I crept into the living room while Dom snored, passed out in the bedroom. I called someone who I knew would reinforce that I had to do the right thing and save myself from this damaged relationship before it destroyed me. I rang Anna, my former high school friend, who was now studying psychology at Sydney University. We hadn't spoken regularly since my life had become a complete mess, and what I had to say came as a shock.

'He hit you?' Anna sounded alarmed. 'Nathan, you must get out of there. No one has the right to do that.'

'I know,' I said quietly with tears running down a bruised chin.

'Are you still there?' Anna asked.

'Yes,' I admitted with a whisper.

'Hang up and get out of there," Anna ordered. 'Now!'

SEXTASY

THE FOLLOWING AFTERNOON, I sat with Anna on the rocks of North Bondi. We'd been talking about what had happened last night. As the waves rolled in, I recounted to my dear high school friend what I'd been through.

'Why didn't you report it to the police?' Anna was outraged the moment I revealed I hadn't gone to the cops.

'Come on, what was I going to do? Walk into Darlinghurst Police Station and say 'my big bad boyfriend' hit me. I can just imagine what their reaction would be. They'd laugh at the poor faggot who was gay bashed by his own boyfriend.'

'No, they wouldn't!' Anna protested. 'What Dom did was assault. It's domestic violence, and you should report it! What if he does it again to someone else?'

'I can't, Anna,' I had to look away from Anna's intense stare. I didn't want to explain the reason I couldn't face the prospect of filing a police report. It was because if I did, it would put Dom behind bars. Dom was still on his good behaviour bond. 'Boy, can I pick them. Tall, handsome, unfaithful, and with a criminal conviction.'

'Yeah, Dom was a real catch!' Anna put her arm around me to comfort me. 'You must end it. Cut Dom off for good.'

'I know, and I will. For real this time.' I nodded and began to pull off the triple-banded Russian wedding ring Dom had given me. It was hard to remove from my ring finger. Just as Dom had been difficult to remove from my life. The ring has been stuck there for so long. For a second, I thought it wasn't going to come off. Suddenly it slipped free, and I held the ring in my fingers. I kissed the ring goodbye, and threw it into the ocean. As the ring sank into the sea, a loud wave crashed against the rocks where Anna and I were sitting.

Responding to the loud clash of the crashing wave Anna smiled. 'How dramatic! It's like the universe just erupted and broke the spell.'

I came to terms that what I thought was the love of my life was an obsession with the completely wrong person. For the first time, it became clear that what I was in love with was the idea of being in love, the comforting sense of having someone to call my own.

After I moved out of Roslyn Place, I learnt Brad had done the same. He didn't want to share an apartment with just Dom. Also, Brad had come to realise Ricky would never be his. Ricky was always looking for someone who could 'keep' him and that wasn't for Brad. Brad and I had both picked lousy love interests. We should have picked each other. It would have made both our lives easier. We were similar types in so many ways. That's what made us friends and not lovers.

Brad had decided to move to the UK to live with Dan in London. 'There's nothing sexual between me and Dan.' Brad assured me. 'There's more modelling opportunities in the UK.'

I couldn't help but be jealous at this news and feared that the two boys I adored could strike up a romantic relationship together in a foreign land. I often found myself wondering how different my life could have been if I'd stayed with Dan on the night of his twenty-first birthday.

A year later, I received a letter from Tiffany with a stamp from a Rome post office. She was living in Italy with her mum and stepdad. She was seeing a local DJ who was helping to produce her music. Her first single did get released but it wasn't a big hit. Going into hiding made promotion of Tiffany's music impossible. Tiffany apologised for all the trouble she'd caused with the stolen credit card. She hoped everything worked out after she left. I was pissed off that she left no return address.

Following my split from Dom, we both endured awkward encounters spotting each other on the Oxford Street scene for years. Generally, we avoided making eye contact across the bar when drinking at Gilligan's, or on the dance floor of the Midnight Shift, and at major dance parties at the Hordern Pavilion such as Mardi Gras and Sleaze Ball. However, on more than one occasion, the morning after, if neither of us had hooked-up with someone new during the night, we'd call each other on the mobile and arrange to have sex.

We barely talked. We just fucked. Our relationship had become all about lust and hate. Even though we both blamed each other for the breakdown of our once obsessive relationship, there was enough desire to keep us entwined in a cycle of loveless sexual encounters, a dance of desperation.

During the last encounter I experienced with Dom, he revealed how he'd met a group of new friends. 'The Fuck Buddies,' Dom called them proudly. It was a group of men he'd met from a phone hook up line who Dom would meet for pre-arranged sex parties. Guys took a combination of ecstasy and Viagra pills, a combo they nick-named sextasy. Then whatever happened, happened, providing it was all safe, or at least that was the idea.

Dom described how *The Fuck Buddies* would take turns and changed condoms for each bottom waiting to be fucked. I was both turned on and horrified by my ex-boyfriend's sexual exploits. It was this revelation that made me stop seeing Dom altogether. I don't think there could ever be enough men in the world to keep Dom satisfied. What chance did I ever have?

A year later, after I graduated from university, I was successful in securing a full-time corporate job and formed a new group of work friends. Unlike Aaron predicted I didn't become a kept man as an easier option.

There were plenty of gay guys where I worked, I made such better quality of friends.

In 1998, my work colleagues and I decided to go to Mardi Gras together as it was shaping up to be one of the biggest parties in years. Dannii Minogue was going perform. I could not wait. True to form, Dom was on the dance floor, moving like he was the centre of a rainbow world. When he noticed me with my attractive work friends, Dom rushed over and gave me a big kiss and a hug. He was so out-of-it that he couldn't see how visibly uncomfortable I was at his advances. I was embarrassed my work mates saw him do this to me.

Most of these work colleagues hadn't seen Dom before. They looked surprised at what they saw, a late-twenty-something-year old, who once may have looked like an Aussie football legend but had now let himself go and was noticeably overweight.

In the years that had passed since I last saw Dom, he had aged beyond his years due to excessive partying.

My openly gay boss and professional mentor Phillip had one thing to say, 'Believe me, Nathan, you can do better!' Phillip just gave me a disapproving look as Dom stood by waiting for me to react.

'Dom, I'm hoping to meet someone new tonight.' I smiled politely.

'Oh!' Dom sounded dumbstruck. 'Sure, me too!' With those words, Dom abruptly moved away and disappeared into the crowded dance floor, leaving me free to make eye contact with the most beautiful young man I'd ever seen. He was even prettier than Brad. Like me, the man was tanned, fit, lean, muscular, dancing shirtless, and covered in sweat. Both being high on ecstasy, no introductions were necessary.

We gravitated towards each other and began kissing the second we came face to face. After kissing passionately, the young man introduced himself. His name was James. James and I spent the night dancing together, kissing and being told by complete strangers what a beautiful couple we made. We both loved the DJ's song choice, The BT & Sasha's Bucklodge Ashram Remix of Madonna's 'Drowned World/Substitute for love'.

The following morning, James invited me to his apartment on Flinders Street where we both took another ecstasy pill and had sex till mid-afternoon, before passing out from exhaustion. Unfortunately, our connection only lasted for a total of three days, just long enough for the drugs to wear off, a classic chemical romance.

I was greatly disappointed when James revealed he was not looking for a long-term boyfriend.

'But we'd be so good together!' I insisted.

'Sorry, sweetheart. I'm happy being single!' James smiled innocently.

Coming down the following week, I was devastated that my chance encounter with James didn't become something more.

I was desperately lonely and still longing to meet my Mr Right. However, meeting James and publicly rejecting Dom on the dance floor was a cathartic experience and helped me to finally move on emotionally. Because of my life experiences, it never occurred to me that one day I might meet someone who was my equal and would complement me in every way possible. Instead, I had a vision that one day, when I was much older, and in my thirties, I'd be the one who walked into a bar and have all the young things who were looking to be a *kept man* competing for my attention. I knew this was a warped view of my possible future, but having come out of a warped relationship, I found it hard to see life clearly. My desire to be the man in control led me to work hard and put my degree to good use. Within another year, I was earning a high income in the marketing department of a large Australian corporation.

All I needed now, was a toy boy.

~

Working hard and no longer partying hard, I was more than comfortable with the fact that I hadn't seen or heard from Dom for several years. Then one day, I got a call from a number I didn't recognise on my mobile in between meetings. Assuming it was a Recruitment Professional I answered it out of curiosity.

'Can I see you?' It was Dom.

'Dom, I'm busy.' I was annoyed at being interrupted at work, especially by my ex who I hadn't spoken to in years. I couldn't believe he still had my mobile number saved in his phone.

'Please, I really need to talk to you!' He sounded distraught.

'What is it? Did you rob a bank?'

'Nathan, this is serious. I need to see you.'

'I can't, Dom. I just can't.'

'Please, I need you now more than ever!'

From the tone in Dom's voice, and knowing the sort of stuff Dom was into, and the way he spoke, I think I guessed what was wrong. I felt stunned. But by this stage of my life, it had been too long since we'd parted to give Dom anymore of myself to someone who'd cost me so much.

'Dom the reason I can see you anymore is because I'm with someone.'

I was firm. I knew that I had to be. 'It wouldn't be appropriate for me to see you now that I'm in a long-term and committed relationship. My partner wouldn't appreciate it if I saw you. He knows all about you.'

'Oh.' Dom was lost for words for the first time I had known him.

Neither of us said anything for a moment.

The silence was increasingly deafening until Dom spoke, 'I don't know why, but I always thought throughout everything we went through that we'd end up together down the line.'

'Better the devil you know.' I agreed. 'For a long time, I thought so too. But I see my future differently these days.'

'Whoever you're with now, I hope he's good to you.'

'He is.'

EPILOGUE

ANY QUESTIONS?

MY FINGERS RESTED on the stop button of my cassette recorder. The tape was near the end.

'Mr James, unless you have anything else to say about your actions, you are free to leave this interview,' Constable First Class Ferguson instructed Dom. 'That is, of course, unless you do have something more you'd like to tell us?'

Dom remained silent.

'As I've told you previously, you're not obliged to say anything unless you wish to do so, but whatever you say will be electronically recorded and may be used in evidence and against you. Do you understand that?'

'I understand,' Dom answered defensively. 'Look, it's like I told you, we just thought it would be a bit of fun. I can't recall what I was thinking at the time. I never thought any harm would come of it.'

www.ingramcontent.com/pod-product-compliance
Lightning Source LLC
Chambersburg PA
CBHW071236130626
46556CB00003B/1040